P9-DJA-185

PRAISE FOR HOOKED

"Wolf, an award-winning filmmaker, has adapted this first novel from his own original screenplay, and its cinematic potential clearly shows. The high-concept narrative is entertaining, well-paced, and highly visual ... It's a charming, humorous, and hopeful tale. A quirky, touching love story that offers insights into autism, religion, and personal tragedy."
- Kirkus Reviews

"A wonderfully well-written, funny, romantic love story. Unique and inspirational. *Hooked* is not your average romance. Rarely do I find myself so captivated by a book that I cannot put it down for nearly two hours. Pick up this book and get lost in the beauty of their relationship. My only complaint would be that the story had an ending, as all stories do, and I did so want to keep reading on. Most highly recommended. *Hooked* is simply remarkable."
- Readers' Favorite

"By turning conventions of contemporary romance on its stilettos and swapping out the typical sassy, fashion-obsessed female protagonist for an autistic male who reads jokes from index cards, Wolf puts a fresh spin on the genre. Adapted from his award-winning screenplay, *Hooked* shows signs of its origins with snappy dialogue and humorous, well-staged scenes ... A sweet and entertaining romantic comedy, *Hooked* touches on autism and the power of faith. It will appeal to any reader who enjoys a blend of quirky characters, humor and drama."
- Blue Ink Review

"Heartfelt, out-of-the-ordinary romance. This warm, witty story does not shy away from serious themes like exploitation, redemption, and true love. *Hooked* explores heavy issues with a light touch. It's easy to see this being adapted into an enjoyable movie."
- Foreword Reviews

PRAISE FOR HOOKED
THE SCREENPLAY THE NOVEL IS BASED UPON

"A very sweet and endearing romantic comedy, with an excellent relationship between Violet and Shawn at the center." — *The Black List*

"A rewardingly nuanced, three-dimensional, and charming– if unconventional–love story. Strong character voices define the entirety of the plot, while the genuine chemistry between the central roles creates a natural, seemingly effortless appeal within both their relationships and their perspectives in broader terms ... Superb characters, strong dialogue, and a polished overall execution wind up rendering a finished product that seems in many ways both moving and entertaining." — *Script Shark*

"Incredible characters and story." — *Cinequest*

"*Hooked* is a sweet, touching story that works to bring out the best in people, using autism as a backdrop."
— *Tracking Board*

"*Hooked* is a fluently written romantic comedy that both acknowledges and deviates from the conventions in a sparky, original manner ... While this set up might seem wildly implausible at first glance, it's established in a very organic way, with warmth, intelligence and wit – three qualities that characterize the rest of the screenplay ... Overall, this screenplay achieves the rare feat of being both funny and romantic, delivering an emotionally satisfying ending to Violet and Shawn's misadventures, without patronizing the audience."
— *BlueCat Screenplay Competition*

"A lot of heart, poignancy and charm." — *Coverage Ink*

HOOKED

ALLEN WOLF

MORNING STAR
PUBLISHING

MORNING STAR
PUBLISHING

Hooked

Written by Allen Wolf, adapted from his screenplay

Kindly direct inquiries about the novel or screenplay to:
info@morningstarpictures.com

www.MorningStar-Publishing.com

Copyright © 2015 Allen Wolf, all rights reserved

All rights reserved. In accordance with the U.S. Copyright Act of 1976, the scanning, uploading, and electronic sharing of any part of this book without the permission of the author constitutes unlawful piracy and theft of the author's intellectual property. If you would like to use material from the book (other than for review purposes), prior written permission must be obtained by contacting the author at info@morningstarpictures.com. Thank you for your support of the author's rights.

Scriptures from the Holy Bible, New International Version ® , NIV ®, Copyright © 1973, 1978, 1984 by Biblica Inc. ™ Used by permission of Zondervan. All rights reserved worldwide. United States Patent and Trademark Office by Biblica Inc. ™

ISBN 978-0-692-38661-3

Underlying Screenplay: "Hooked"

Screenplay © 2015, Allen Wolf, all rights reserved.

Published in the United States of America. First Edition

For my loving wife Ramesh
and my daughter Adele.
You are precious gifts to me.

This is also dedicated to
those caught in human trafficking.
May you experience freedom, healing and grace.

CONTENTS

Acknowledgments   i

ACKNOWLEDGMENTS

I'm very grateful to all the terrific people
whose support helped make this story possible –
Scot & Kelly Barton, Eric Bischoff & Nejat Abduljelil,
Chris & Carrie Cavigioli, Brown & Eileen Councill,
Tom & Katie Eggemeier, Neil and Dana Gamblin,
Vincent & Jennifer Granson Lee, Karen Johnson,
Eric & Susan Metaxas, Sam & Cindy Moser,
Peter and Amanda Trautmann, Michael Uhl,
Jim & Carol VanArtsdalen and Lou & Faith Vision.

Thank you Patricia Beauchamp, Matt Fury,
Adam Levenberg, Tom Rice, Minna Kim
and George Verongos
for your helpful contributions.

Thank you CAST (Coalition to Abolish Slavery &
Trafficking) and NightLight International
for your insight and efforts to end trafficking.

I'm thankful for my family, friends and community and all
the friendly cast members at Disneyland who encouraged
me during my weekly writing sessions at the park.

CHAPTER 1

IT'S STORMY

Tree branches swayed in the wind, colliding against each other with a clang, clung, clang sound, like wind chimes on a blustery day. The petals of the red snapdragons circling the trunks of the trees shivered in the wind, sounding like sustained chords of a violin. Sunlight sparkled off the water feature next to the flowers, delivering ding, ding, tinkle, tinkle noises as it flowed down the length of the path.

"Are you even listening?"

Shawn broke out of his trance and peered over at Cheryl, who walked beside him, her head cocked to the side, wondering where he'd been.

She was nice-looking but unremarkable, stuck in a body the height of a redwood tree. It was hard for Shawn to look into her eyes, or anyone's eyes for that matter. When he did, it felt like he was looking into the sun itself. He forced himself to do it, though, knowing it made people uneasy when he kept looking away. But he couldn't keep it up for long. The connection felt too electric, as though he was sticking his finger into a wall socket.

They were walking through High Line Park that snaked above 11th Avenue, formerly abandoned railroad tracks that were transformed into a popular park years ago. The azure sky above peeked out from behind the low hanging clouds that kissed the Manhattan skyscrapers. This was Shawn's favorite spot for dates, though the cacophony of sounds from all the colors pounded inside his mind.

Shawn had powder blue eyes, a trim physique, and a handsome, well-shaped face crowned with sandy blond hair. He had never quite grown into his long arms and legs. When he walked, it sometimes looked like he was carefully stepping between raindrops, especially when he started noticing all the colors around him. At twenty-four years old, he didn't yet feel like an adult.

"Hello?" Cheryl said, knocking on an invisible door between them.

Shawn pulled himself back into reality. "Sorry. I get distracted sometimes." He looked up at her height. "You must be good at basketball."

Her eyes narrowed onto him. This wasn't his first awkward comment of the night. "You must be great at miniature golf."

"I'm really not."

"You gonna ask me how the weather is up here? I'll save you the trouble." She popped the cap off her bottle and splashed water on his face. "It's stormy."

"I didn't mean to offend you." Shawn assured Becky on a different date. She was in her thirties, lean and frail looking, friendly but needy. She wore rainbow suspenders covered in buttons with pictures of cats. Shawn had just finished relaying a fact about cats sleeping for seventy percent of their lives.

Becky thought he was being judgmental. "Cats have feelings too, you know."

Shawn nodded impatiently, wondering when this date would end. "You look different from your profile picture," he remarked.

She smiled uneasily. "Confession time. That's actually my sister. I get a lot more interest when I use her pic."

"Well, she is a lot prettier than you."

Becky shrank back, wondering if she heard him right.

Shawn's thoughts often raced out of his mouth, unedited. He felt like a car driving fifty miles an hour down the highway. Most people could speed by him or change lanes, but all he could do was keep going fifty and people had to get used to that or drive away. Most sped off, including Becky.

"I didn't say that right," Shawn informed Lindsay on his latest date, which was going surprisingly well. They ambled down the path together. She was in her twenties, with delicate features and dark hair pulled back from the planes of her face.

Shawn fought to keep his thoughts on track. "Our cone cells determine our sensitivity to what we see." Then, he forced himself to stop talking, a skill his grandmother taught him that usually led people to talk with him longer.

Lindsay leaned into him as they strolled, clearly taken by his show of knowledge. "That's so fascinating. You're like a walking Wikipedia."

Shawn beamed. He searched for a new topic to unearth, something even more enthralling. "I read an article the other day about how this place would still be abandoned railroad tracks if someone didn't have the imagination to see it could be beautiful."

"That's so true."

"When it opened, they called it a secret, magic garden in the sky." He started walking with a spring in his step, enjoying the moment. She gently reached out and took hold of his hand. He immediately shook her off, to her surprise.

Shawn looked down and felt the shame creeping in. He wondered if he should tell her what she'd find out eventually. "I'm sorry. Sometimes touching can be too intense…with my autism."

Whenever Shawn told someone about his autism, their reactions were a mysterious mixed bag. Mysterious because he couldn't tell what they were thinking. Though he did notice those dates usually didn't last very long after he brought this information to light, even when he explained he was high functioning. His brother Colin thought Shawn should keep his autism a secret for as long as possible, or at least until the second date. But whenever Shawn kept those details in the dark, his dates seemed confused by how he would react to bright sunlight, a loud sound, someone touching him, or various other situations.

Shawn's own parents weren't happy with his diagnosis; his brother told him that to explain their absence. They suspected something was different about Shawn when he was two years old and lining up his toys in a perfectly neat row, according to size. Then when he turned three, he stopped talking or looking people in their eyes. He also flapped his hands a lot. When his parents tried to give him a hug, he pushed them away. They took Shawn to a doctor who diagnosed him as being autistic.

Shawn's mother cried the rest of that afternoon while his father walked down to the bar at the end of the street. It had a broken neon sign and a skinny bartender who called him "hon" while handing him drink after drink with nicotine-stained fingers.

Shawn's grandparents were convinced he could be helped with the right therapy and they made that case to his skeptical parents. After several unsuccessful trips to a program in their area, where Shawn ended up yelling uncontrollably and hiding in a corner of the room, his parents were ready to give up, but not his grandparents. They offered to transfer Shawn into a program in Manhattan that was experimental but seeing results.

The trips to get treatment in the city and the constant "homework" left his parents little time to fix their own marriage, which was struggling in sinking sand ever since they brought Colin into the world.

Shawn's condition was tearing at the seams of their marriage, or at least that was the excuse they used to convince his grandparents to let Shawn live with them. Colin couldn't stop crying when Shawn was no longer around so he soon joined his brother in the city.

After Shawn and Colin moved away, their parents trekked into the city to see them on the weekends. After a while, they started skipping a weekend here and there and, eventually, whole months altogether. Colin could tell his grandparents weren't happy with their absence and overheard them use words like "disappointing," "hurt," and "abandoned" when they spoke in tense sentences to their son over the phone.

Shawn and Colin started to miss their parents less and less as their grandparents filled their shoes. Colin eventually concluded that he and Shawn were keeping their parents from the life they really wanted. He could also smell alcohol on his dad's breath whenever they did successfully arrange a family get-together.

Lindsay's expression turned from inquisitive to sour on hearing about Shawn's autism. "Oh."

"You look like you swallowed a lemon."

Lindsay shifted her weight and checked her watch. "I just remembered. I need to meet someone. Sorry to cut this short."

"Who do you need to meet?"

She flashed him a toothy smile. "It was so nice meeting you."

"Should we go out again? I like how you smell like laundry detergent." He immediately realized he shouldn't have mentioned her scent. His brother constantly reminded him to keep olfactory observations to himself.

"I'll call you, okay?" she answered, stepping back from him and keeping up her smile.

"I'll wait for your call." Shawn replied, certain that day was just around the corner.

Her plastered smile continued unchanged as she made her way down a nearby stairway to the lively street below.

As Shawn watched her leave, he noticed all the colors around him roar back to life. The clanging tree branches, humming violin petals, and tinkling water pressed into his mind as the evening sun became dazzlingly bright. Shawn shielded his eyes and rapidly left in the other direction, on his way home.

Home for Shawn was on the upper west side of Manhattan inside a large condo he shared with his grandmother. The kitchen, dining room, and living room all enjoyed the same connected space and a partial view of Central Park. Hanging on the silver-gray walls were black and white oil paintings of scenes from the city—wet seals basking in the sun at the Central Park Zoo, the triangular Flatiron building dominating its street corner, a couple caught in intimate conversation in front of a boxy florist shop in SoHo. All were proud creations of Shawn's grandmother, Ruth, whose spotless home would feel more like a museum if the furniture ever went missing.

A gold birdcage took up residence in the corner of the room near the window. Inside, the yellow and green lovebirds, Sunny and Cloudy, nestled against each other. Shawn dropped a large spoonful of cooked lentils into their feeding trough. His grandmother liked to stick her fingers into the cage to caress their feathers, but not Shawn. Feeding them was the closest he wanted to get.

He kicked his feet up onto the walnut coffee table and tried to sink into the red velvet couch but it never let him. It was too much like his grandmother, stiff and proper. He was watching a black and white movie about a woman about to get married to the love of her life. She tried on different wedding dresses until one transformed her homely appearance into something regal.

Ruth's voice echoed from her bedroom down the hall. "Shawn, I can hear your feet on the table."

"You can't hear feet," Shawn returned. But he quickly moved them off the table, just in case.

Ruth glided into the room in a vintage 1940s robe. She was in her seventies with curly auburn hair and a slim body, a gift from her years of swimming. There was something stately about her that sometimes masked her artistic side. She never travelled anywhere without *putting her face on*, as she'd call it. "Bore me with all the details," she commanded him.

Shawn looked away from her, not wanting to. He wished there were other possibilities on the horizon but the sun was always setting on his dating life. She kept poking him for an answer. "It went the same as always..." he confessed. And then he changed the subject. "I was thinking about Grandpa."

"Yeah?"

"The way he died. So suddenly. I don't want that to happen to you."

"That's sweet, Shawn," she said, walking toward him. She took an unsteady step and grabbed a nearby chair to get her balance.

"I don't know who would buy my cereal or help me pay bills or..."

"Glad I'll be missed," she said with a wry smile, knowing he didn't have a filter.

Shawn returned his attention to the TV. Sometimes at night, he would think about the day when his grandmother would no longer be there and that usually meant he would toss and turn in bed for a few hours. It didn't help that his grandpa passed away a year earlier. It was so sudden and unexpected. He woke up that morning to his grandfather giving him his favorite cereal and retired to bed to the cries of his grandma in her room next to his.

Colin didn't go to their grandpa's funeral. Not because he didn't love him. He couldn't handle all the overwhelming feelings ever since Shawn told Colin that Grandpa was with Jesus now.

Grandpa took the place in their hearts their own father was supposed to fill and they loved him for that. Grandpa was also a jokester. He'd ask them about their day and then pretend to turn off his hearing aid. Or he'd ask them if they saw that grown up Smurf movie. When they didn't know what he was talking about he'd tell them the title—*Avatar*. Once he told them the best part of growing up was less and less peer pressure since all his peers were dying off.

Colin's absence at the funeral quickly became a sore spot between him and Ruth. Even more so when she found out where he actually went that evening— the Comedy Cellar. Colin always thought that was the best way to honor his grandpa.

On the TV, the woman was dolled up for her big day, gliding down a sweeping staircase toward her striking groom, who was smiling ear to ear. Shawn imagined himself as that groom, waiting for the love of his life to commit herself to him forever. It gave him goose bumps just thinking about it.

"Can you tell me about your wedding day again, Grandma?"

Ruth didn't answer. Shawn looked over and saw her slumped in her chair, looking like a marionette without its strings. "Grandma?"

His mouth dried up. His heartbeat quickened. He rushed over to her. Shook her. She flopped around in his hands.

CHAPTER 2

PICKY ABOUT THE GUESTS

Shawn held onto the metal bar on the inside of the ambulance as it raced across town toward Mt. Sinai Hospital. He watched the brawny paramedic insert an IV into his grandmother's arm as she lay still on the stretcher. He shut his ears to the piercing whup, whup of the ambulance siren.

Hours later, Shawn wrung his hands as he sat in a chair next to his grandma, praying silently. She was asleep in her hospital bed in a room she shared with a frail woman who needed a machine to breathe. A pale yellow curtain separated them. Ruth looked fragile in her sea foam colored hospital gown, under the loud fluorescent lights. The air felt still and was quiet, except for the beeps and woosh sounds from the various machines surrounding her bed.

A short doctor entered the room with Ruth's chart and stood next to him. He was a sturdy man with deep-set eyes and graying hair, in his late forties with a kind face behind round glasses. He wore boots, probably to give himself some extra height. "When you get to her age, things start breaking down fast," he explained with a sigh.

Shawn shushed him. "Praying." The doctor nodded impatiently. After a moment, Shawn raised his head to indicate the doctor could continue.

Before he could, the sizable white door to the room swung open and Shawn's brother, Colin, rushed inside. Colin was in his thirties, with a narrow face and spiky blond hair; scruffy and easygoing to the point of not doing much with his life. He started to give Shawn a hug but stopped himself. "Panic attack?" he asked them.

"Diabetes. Her blood sugar was too low. She passed out," Shawn told him.

"She needs to carefully monitor herself to stay healthy. Especially at her age," the doctor added.

"That's what they said to Grandpa before he went to sleep and didn't wake up," Shawn returned.

"Did he also have diabetes?"

Shawn and Colin both nodded. They could hear their grandfather in their heads, reminding them that when life hands you lemons, diabetics should not make lemonade. Grandpa also liked to say the reason he married Grandma was because she was his "type." Type 1 diabetes.

"Well, you've got to take it one day at a time. We can release her tomorrow," the doctor told them before unleashing familiar facts and tips about diabetes.

Colin motioned to the patient on the other side of the curtain. "I heard that woman swallowed a hundred dollar bill."

The doctor glanced at the woman and then back to Colin, confused.

Colin leaned in. "Has there been any change?"

Colin laughed but the doctor shook his head and made his way out of the room.

"Was that a joke?" Shawn asked him.

"This is exactly when we need jokes. You know Grandpa would be cracking a few."

Shawn pulled the covers closer to Ruth's neck, tucking her in. "If we lose Grandma—"

"Like the doctor said. One day at a time, Shawn."

"I always thought I'd get married before she passed away."

"Better hurry up then." Colin said with a twinkle in his eyes. Shawn glared at him. "I'm kidding. Kidding. But, I'm kind of not kidding, too."

"I asked a girl to go out this weekend. She told me she was going to have a headache."

"I'll give you some pointers."

"I need more than that."

"Doesn't your work help out in that department?"

"Not as much as I thought it would."

Shawn landed his job at Exclusively Yours, an elite dating website, thinking it would skyrocket his possibilities of finding his future wife, but he felt stuck on the launching pad. It was rare for him to get past the first date and when he did, it was unlikely he'd be granted another one.

He was always the first one at his cubicle every day. He liked getting to the office before everyone else so he could organize his desk, push in his earplugs, and get busy writing code for the site distraction-free.

When he arrived early, he sometimes said "Hello" to the pictures of the freakishly happy couples plastered on the walls around the office. He stopped doing that, right after he heard a "Hello" back from someone who had beat him to the office. Shawn was the butt of a few jokes during that day's lunch break.

Taped to the inside walls of Shawn's cubicle were neatly arranged pictures of happily married couples he had cut out from different magazines or printed from his favorite wedding websites. In one photo, a groom carried his bride across the threshold of their front door. In another, a married couple locked lips on the end of a pier. Another snapshot featured a newly hitched couple waving from the backseat of a taxi. All those scenes gave him hope.

Sometimes, Shawn would close his eyes and pretend he was the man in those pictures. Then he'd lose track of the time. One morning, he even nodded off. So, he only allowed himself to imagine that when he felt especially lonely.

The employees in the other cubicles around him were good-looking, mostly in their twenties, and they frequently met up for drinks after work and failed to invite Shawn. They took calls all day and masked their socializing and gaming as work.

When Shawn first started working there, he tried to work up conversations with them. He'd force himself to look into their eyes while he came up with interesting facts about dating sites or love in general. Before long, they didn't have time to talk to him and it became too much work for him to try to connect. He resorted to a quick "hello" in the elevator and they were fine with that.

Jammed between two of the pictures on his cubicle was one of Shawn's favorite verses from the Bible written across a blue index card – "I waited patiently for the Lord; He turned to me and heard my cry." The card was a note to him from Amanda, whom he dated in college. She was his only relationship that lasted past the second date.

Shawn liked being isolated in his corner cubicle. His desk was always clutter-free, which kept him focused on typing code into his computer to keep the site running smoothly. He was always dressed in a plain polo and jeans—his standard outfit. He had a variety of shirt colors and rotated them; blue was Monday, green Tuesday, orange Wednesday, purple Thursday, gray Friday. Then, he'd repeat them. He stayed away from the more intense colors because their sounds could overpower him.

Out of the corner of his eye, Shawn peered at Flynn, who was sitting a few feet away in all his headphone-wearing, hipster glory, wearing a plaid shirt and skinny jeans. The women in the office seemed to pass by his desk the most. Shawn watched as Flynn scrolled through photos of females on the site.

Their boss, Jake, emerged from his office a few doors down the hall from them. In his late forties, Jake's smile resembled the Cheshire cat. He was tall and toned but tried too hard to look young, tan, and current. He approached Flynn while Shawn pulled out his earplugs to listen in. Jake motioned to the many female faces flashing by on Flynn's computer. "Flynn, my man. How fresh is the meat?"

Flynn's face wrinkled with disappointment. "It's pretty rotten."

Jake watched the screen and grimaced as imperfect women zipped by. "Maybe we should just be a free-for-all and let ugly people mate like everyone else. They're people, too. Aren't they?"

Flynn shrugged.

What made Exclusively Yours so exclusive was how they monitored the offerings and booted anyone out who didn't fit the website's ideals, or more accurately, Jake's ideals. It was a badge of honor if you were accepted by the site and something you didn't mention if you weren't.

A picture of a well-endowed ex-cheerleader type caught Jake's attention. "Who's this hottie?" He asked, clicking on her profile. Below her picture was a red number six. He turned to Shawn. "Why is she rated a six?"

Shawn moved closer to Flynn's computer and glanced at the screen. "Because she lied in her bio."

Jake looked back at the computer, then at Shawn. "How did your system figure that out?"

"She says she majored in cosmetology. At Harvard. Not possible. It cross checks personal data against public records and analyzes—"

Jake interrupted. "And you wonder why we haven't launched your ratings system yet? No one should get a history rating that low with looks like that."

"The score is objective. Based on internet activity, credit score—"

"You better make that kind of look count for something. Otherwise, who cares about people's histories if we lose all the hot and young with valid credit cards?" Shawn acknowledged he had a point and Jake returned to his office.

"Um, my account was erased again," Shawn mentioned to Flynn.

"Oh, yeah. New rule. Employees can't use our site anymore," Flynn explained.

"But you are."

"For quality control."

"What about Adele?"

"Uh, same thing."

"And José?"

Flynn frowned. "Shawn, I'm sorry. We've had a few complaints from the girls you met. Actually, all the girls you met."

Shawn's expression turned to concern.

Flynn softened. "Not a big deal. But maybe you can try some other sites."

"I know my chances of finding someone will go up if I can—"

"Sorry, man," Flynn said with a huff, turning back to his computer and snapping his headphones back on.

Shawn wondered if he should say anything else, then decided to let it go for now. Knowing he could get fixated on what he thought was important, he returned to his desk, feeling an ache in the pit of his stomach. He was either hungry or lonely. Or both.

Tammy made her way through the cubicles, dropping off envelopes. She was in her mid-twenties, pretty but edgy, blond with streaks of a darker color, hiding her looks under the causes she preached about. That day's shirt read 'FUR is Dead'. She handed Flynn an envelope. "Passes for the women haters' ball."

"You mean work party?" Flynn asked.

"Open your eyes."

Tammy was used to that kind of reaction from her coworkers whenever she woke them up with a splash of reality. She felt like she was the only one who cared about what was really happening in the world. When others complained about the cost of a gym membership, she complained about the lack of clean water in Africa.

When Tammy first started working at Exclusively Yours, they invited her out to drinks but she wanted to keep a safe distance. When people asked her how she met Jake and where she worked previously, she turned the conversation into what they could do to make the world a better place. Soon, rumors started flying around the office about how and why she hired.

Shawn glanced up at Tammy, looking hopeful for an invite. She kept walking. "Sorry, Shawn. Jake is picky about the guests."

"What if I don't eat or drink anything?" Shawn asked, looking like a dog begging for scraps.

Tammy looked him over and pity got the better of her. She snuck an envelope to Shawn, while putting on a show for the benefit of her co-workers. "Can't do it, Shawn. You know when Jake says 'no', he means 'no'." She stared daggers at the others in the office. "Kind of like victims of sexual assault. No means no, people!"

Shawn could hear a few groans around the office. This wasn't her first mini lecture. He looked between the envelope and Tammy, confused. "If I can't go, who's this for?"

Tammy moved close enough to Shawn so the others couldn't hear. He could smell her musk perfume but didn't say anything. "I hate the theme and object to it on principle, but I hope to see you there. You can bring a guest but avoid Jake and make sure you're in costume." She started to say more but stopped herself.

Shawn pulled the invite out of the envelope and examined the puffy 1970s style font that announced Pimps and Hos Party! The only way he could go was if he didn't tell his grandma the theme. She had returned from the hospital after being held overnight for observation.

Colin reluctantly stepped into her role while she was gone but mixed up the order of his morning so Shawn was glad to have Grandma back. She didn't like talking about her hospital visit and Shawn was fine to let the topic alone. There was no need to bring up a Pimps and Hos party. She might get upset. So he'd have to tell her he was off to a work party. She'll be happy to know it's a chance for him to meet someone special.

CHAPTER 3

PIMPS AND HOS

Shawn stood next to the curb in front of a large warehouse where techno music boomed. Before he left his grandma's apartment, she made him promise to be careful, while placing his hand on the family Bible. Whenever Shawn caught Grandpa reading that same Bible, he'd always announce he was "looking for loopholes." But Shawn knew better. Every Sunday, his grandparents faithfully attended church and now Shawn took his grandpa's place.

Men and women dressed as pimps and hos from the 1970s passed by Shawn and lined up at the entrance to the warehouse. A burly man dressed head to toe in black leather took their passes and opened the velvet rope to allow people inside. Shawn was dressed in a ruby smoking jacket. The Manhattan

Bridge stretched majestically overhead with the city as its jeweled backdrop.

"What's up, bro?"

Shawn turned to see Colin dressed in a shimmery gold suit, white platform shoes, giant glasses, and a feathered hat. "This is a pimps and hos party. Why are you dressed like Elton John?"

Colin looked over his get up and realized he did look like Elton John. He shrugged and pointed to Shawn's outfit. "So says the man dressed as..."

"Hugh Hefner. He's the ultimate pimp." Shawn beamed proudly. "I read that online."

Colin and Shawn made their way through the crush of people inside the party, past the colorful pimps and hos who mingled around the warehouse, shouting to be heard above the music. The women wore a range of styles, from tight mini skirts to barely anything at all, complimented with fishnet or torn stockings, stilettos or thigh high boots. The men were dressed in colorful suits with bell-bottom pants, some donning oversized Afro wigs. One of the men kept his 'hos' on a studded leash, which was disturbing to Shawn.

Shawn tried to strike up conversations with several different women when Colin left to use the restroom. The chitchat didn't last long. One woman walked away in the middle of him telling her captivating facts about the internal combustion engine.

Another lady told Shawn she needed to meet up with a friend across the room. When he turned to see who she met up with, she was standing alone next to the bar, checking her phone. Undaunted, he struck up a conversation with another woman who simply said, "no hablo Inglés," before he overheard her talking to someone else in English.

After Colin returned, Tammy approached them, dressed in a slim black dress featuring a bright graphic of a traffic light. "You look like a stoplight," Shawn told her, stating the obvious.

Tammy nodded, glad he noticed. "Exactly. Stop human trafficking. That's my message."

Shawn looked over her dress, confused. "What does that have to do—"

"You think 'hos' are 'hos' by choice? Is it a choice if you can't stop the sexual abuse you got as a kid? Why are we celebrating women being trafficked by pimps?"

"You're kind of intense," Colin informed her.

"Modern slavery is intense," Tammy returned, then she flashed a smile. "Enjoy the party." She disappeared into the crowd.

Shawn and Colin gave each other a shrug and continued onward, toward the bar at the center of the room.

As Shawn looked around, the room felt like it was going to engulf him. The music became excessively loud. The swirling, colored lights beaming down from the ceiling seemed to grow brighter. The voices and music fused together and became deafening. Shawn started wringing his hands and gazed off into the distance.

Colin noticed Shawn zoning out. "You okay, bro?"

Shawn forced a smile. Colin handed him earplugs. "Just breathe. Concentrate on one thing at a time. Free food, free drinks, lots of eye candy. Feels like Christmas to me." Three ladies in tight, revealing outfits sashayed by them and caught Colin's attention. "Ho, ho, and ho."

Shawn noticed them too, concerned. "The way these women are dressed will increase chances of unwanted pregnancy."

Colin laughed. He liked how Shawn would point out what others noticed but would never say.

Jake approached the bar in a red velvet suit and gold chains. Shawn turned away from him but not quickly enough.

"Shawn?"

Shawn nervously walked away but Jake quickly caught up to him. "I'm not eating or drinking," he informed him awkwardly.

"It's okay. Relax. I never thought you'd want to attend our par-tays. You get mad when we breathe too loud."

"Can't find my soul mate if I just sit at home."

Jake glanced around the room. "Well, you're surrounded by oysters. Go find your pearl."

"My pearl?"

Jake groaned impatiently, then reached for his wallet. He waved a one hundred dollar bill. "Let's make this interesting. This is yours if you get a date with any of these hos."

Colin approached. "Easy money."

"Oh yeah? So it's a bet?"

Colin winked at Shawn. "Sure."

Jake smiled, satisfied, and walked off.

Shawn looked over to Colin, a little afraid. "That's a lot of money."

"I'm up for a challenge." That moment brought back memories of Atlantic City. On his twenty-first birthday, Colin thought it would be fun to trek out to the casinos to try his luck at blackjack. Not exactly luck. He was hoping Shawn could count the cards and tell him when to say, "Hit me." He got the idea from watching *Rain Man*. But it turned out Shawn didn't have those same skills. Colin spent the rest of the weekend searching for quiet places where Shawn wouldn't feel deluged by all the lights and activity.

Colin peered around the room for a possible candidate for Shawn. "What about her?" Colin pointed to a tall, curvy woman with chestnut hair who leaned against the wall, sipping her drink. She glanced their way. Colin caught her eye and nodded. "She's kinda flirty. Turn on your charm."

Shawn stood there, not sure what to do.

Colin nudged him impatiently. "Smile back."

Shawn smiled big. Way too big.

"No. Stop. Get her attention, don't make her think you're running for office. Try something more subtle. Like this." A faint smile spread across Colin's lips.

Shawn mirrored Colin's smile and pivoted toward the woman. Except he kept smiling as though he was hatching an evil plan. Colin waved at him to stop. "Creepy. Creepy. Don't smile the whole time. Just long enough to hook her, not make her blow the rape whistle."

From his silence, Shawn didn't appear to know how long that was supposed to be. Colin understood. "Three seconds tops. Turn your head, smile for three seconds, then turn back. Try it."

Shawn took a breath and set his watch. He turned his head, smiled, started the timer—1 ... 2 ... 3 ... He turned his head back. Dropped the smile. Colin beamed. "That was amazing."

Together, they glanced over to the woman. Her mouth was agape. She was either thoroughly creeped out or horrified; it was hard to tell. She quickly dovetailed into the crowd. Colin's shoulders slumped in defeat. "Well, what's a hundred dollars?"

Shawn kept scanning the crowd; he wasn't ready to give up. He saw a few faces and tried the three-second smile with no results.

Then he saw her.

She was in her early twenties with jet-black hair tickling her shoulders. She had a beautiful, angular face and eyes the color of jade. Her face resembled the woman in the old movie he was watching the other night. She was dressed in a white velvet tube top, tiny white skirt, and thigh high white boots. She wore heavy makeup to make her look older, harder, but there was a glimmer of sweetness there.

Shawn waved to her and did his three second smile. She stopped and realized he was smiling at her. She started walking toward him. It worked! Colin noticed her approaching and gave Shawn a friendly push toward her before stepping away.

She reached Shawn and gave him a nod and a wink. Shawn pointed to her white tube top. "White is the color of all wavelengths of visible light. People think black is all colors but black is the absence of color."

She tilted her head, curious. "Uh huh. I'm Violet."

Shawn stood a little taller. "A color on the higher end of the visible spectrum. I'm Shawn. Would you like to go on a date with me?"

Violet laughed. "You always that quick?" She ran her fingers through her hair as she looked him over. "We can go someplace right now."

"I can't right now."

"We can do later but it'll cost you." Violet gave him a sly wink. "You're at a pimps and hos party. Talking to a 'ho.'"

He shook his head, confused. "I'm not good at pretend."

"And I'm good at everything as long as I'm paid by the hour."

"I used to be paid by the hour. Now I'm on salary."

"Three hundred an hour. But I promise I'm worth it."

Shawn's eyes opened wide with curiosity. "What do you do to earn that much?"

"Like I said. Everything," Violet declared, licking her upper lip. Shawn wondered if she was thirsty.

He thought through his week. "You free Saturday night?"

She moved a little closer to him. He could smell her minty breath as she traced the opening of her tube top with her fingers. "What time?"

"I don't know. 7:00?"

"Until when?"

"10?"

Violet looked him over and batted her eyelashes. "Big spender."

"Not really. If we lasted that long, it'll be a new record for me."

"Not for me. Text me your address."

She handed him a business card. It was white and only said Violet with a phone number and an email. He took it and smiled back at her, feeling accomplished. "I look forward to going out."

"Going somewhere is extra."

"Oh. Then we can stay in. My grandma can make us something."

"Your grandma will be there?"

"She'll be happy to see you. I hope that's okay."

"I've never done that before but whatever." She gave him another wink and a seductive lip lick. "I'll bring dessert."

"I like chocolate," he told her, blankly.

Violet nodded and couldn't understand why he didn't react like other men did to her advances. Most guys would've left the party with her right away. This one had a patience she hadn't seen before.

She turned and got lost in the crowd. As Shawn watched her go, the music roared back into his mind. The lights around him sparkled brightly, like miniature suns floating throughout the room.

Colin approached him, pleased. "Hey, bro. We won a hundred bucks."

Shawn couldn't care less about the money. He had something much better. A date.

CHAPTER 4

THE GIRLFRIEND EXPERIENCE

Shawn's grandma was in overdrive to make this date a success. She wore an apron over her silk nightgown and hustled around the kitchen, putting spices into a pot of boiling chili on the stove. This was the first time she had a front row seat for one of Shawn's dates and she took a long afternoon nap so she'd be at the top of her game.

"Plates. Forks, knives, spoons, napkins," she mumbled to herself. "What else? What else?"

"You're sure chili is the way to go, Grandma?"

"It's hearty. Healthy. Easy to eat. It's what your grandpa and I had on our first date. Of course, it was in the middle of a blizzard. Just make sure you keep looking into her eyes. Women like that."

Shawn looked away from her. "I'll do my best."

Ruth handed Shawn drinking glasses that he carefully placed on the table.

Knock. Knock.

Ruth rushed to the door and opened it carefully to find Violet wearing a tank top, tight purple skirt, fishnet stockings and a pair of impossible heels, carrying a knock off Louis Vuitton bag and a long coat.

"You must be the grandma. I thought he was joking," Violet said, biting her lower lip.

"It's hard for me to joke," Shawn yelled from the kitchen.

"Women certainly dress edgy these days," Ruth returned, her eyes narrowing on Violet's wardrobe.

Violet let herself into the living room and put her coat at the edge of the couch. "I've never done anything like this before."

"Anything like what?" Ruth asked.

"I have rules." Violet told them, rubbing her hands together. "No touching until I say it's okay. And if I don't want to do something, I won't. No pictures and no tweeting."

"I wouldn't even know how," Ruth told Violet with a wink. "Most women today have terrible boundaries. I like you already. I'm off to bed. You and Shawn go ahead and enjoy each other."

"We will," Violet told her as she twisted the ring on her finger.

"I hope to see you soon." Ruth kissed Shawn on his cheek and retreated to her bedroom at the end of the hall. Violet's eyes darted around the room.

"Did you forget dessert?" Shawn asked, puzzled.

"It's right here," Violet told him, motioning to herself.

Shawn didn't know how to respond so he ushered her over to the table.

"Dinner? You were serious."

"People tell me I can be too serious."

Violet nods. "You want the girlfriend experience."

"As long as it leads to something more."

"Oh, it will. We can role-play whatever you want."

"Are you hungry?" Shawn asked.

Violet's voice dropped a register, into sultry zone. "I'm very hungry." She picked up a muffin and held it gently between her hands. "Ooooh, muffins. I bet you'd like to see my muffin." She took a long seductive lick of the corn muffin and gently bit into it, winking at him.

"You wink a lot."

She suddenly felt ridiculous and wasn't sure why she grabbed the muffin. She usually had a whole routine she went through with new clients and baked goods were not a part of it. Something was off about their interaction and she didn't know what. She put the muffin back on the table and made her way down the hallway while Shawn watched, completely baffled by her. "I'll let you know when I'm ready."

Plump bride and groom bobbleheads peered out from the shelf above Shawn's desk in his highly organized room. They were a Christmas gift from Colin from years ago, though Shawn had since taped the back of their heads to keep them from constantly nodding. Board games and comic books were stacked on his desk. Computer programming books lined the wall above his bed.

Shawn's favorite game, *You're Pulling My Leg!*, was contained inside a colorful tin lunch box. One of the key game pieces was a box of cards with over six hundred get-to-know-you questions. Shawn often tucked a few game cards into his pocket when he went on a date, to give himself ideas on how to keep the conversation moving.

Violet shook her head at a picture of Ruth with her arm around Shawn in a frame at the end of the shelf, dreading what was to come.

She picked up an ant farm kit from his desk and looked at the tunnels the ants had burrowed into the sand. "You like ants?" she shouted to him.

"They can carry fifty times their weight. Very productive." Shawn yelled from the living room.

Violet pulled back the Star Wars sheets on his twin bed, took a small bottle of perfume from her bag and sprayed a few puffs into the air. She whipped off her tank top, revealing a snake tattoo down her back. "We should get the business part out of the way first."

She turned away from the door to put the perfume back in her purse as Shawn walked in. "The business part?"

At the sight of her naked back, his jaw dropped. He darted his eyes away and backed into the desk, knocking the groom bobblehead off the shelf and dislodging the tape. He caught it and used it to shield his eyes. "I'm so sorry, I didn't know you were changing."

The way he held the bobblehead made it look like it was talking. An amused smile spread across Violet's face as Shawn nervously made his way out of the room. She put her top back on. For once, she was going too quickly.

Shawn rushed to the kitchen sink and splashed water onto his face.

Violet returned to the living room, looking at him through her long eyelashes. "You're new at this. I get it. You booked me for three hours, handsome. We've got some time. But before we begin, I need nine hundred."

Shawn turned to her with a blank look on his face. "Nine hundred what?"

Violet looked him over. "Are you a cop?"

"I'm a computer programmer. For a dating website. I turn original formulations into executable programs, solve problems resulting in an algorithm, verification of requirements of the algorithm including its correctness and its resource consumption, implementation of the algorithm—"

"I'd love to hear more about the algorithms later," Violet told him, tapping her fingers impatiently on her leg.

"I'd really have to show you."

"You're the one who hired me. You can show me whatever you want." Violet started to get nervous. When her clients stalled, bad things usually happened. She had to get her john to pay otherwise she was the one who would pay later.

Shawn looked at her intently. "I don't understand. Why would I hire you?"

Stepping over to the table, Shawn spooned chili into her bowl. She watched him, trying to figure him out. "You mean this was an actual date?"

Shawn straightened. "Of course it's a date. What else would it be?"

Violet took in the setting—the table, the candles, the food. She looked at him and tilted her head, as though suddenly realizing something was different about him. "What do you think I am?"

Shawn shifted uncomfortably, not sure what she was asking. "You're a woman. A pretty woman."

Violet peered into his eyes for a moment, affected by him. He couldn't hold her look for long.

She had been in situations before when the john pretended he didn't know what was going on, sometimes to get out of paying her and other times out of guilt. But this guy was different. He seemed genuinely perplexed.

Shawn helped himself to a muffin. "I can tell you really like muffins. Apple is the official muffin for New York State."

Violet snapped back to reality and typed something into her phone. Shawn watched her, realizing something had changed but he wasn't sure what. "You don't believe me?"

"No, I need to let my guy know what's going on."

"Your guy?"

Violet finished texting. She heard a chirp and noticed the covered cage in the corner of the room. "Pets?"

"Sunny and Cloudy."

"Excuse me?"

"Two lovebirds.

"Real lovebirds?"

Shawn nodded. "When Cloudy threw up, we figured out he was the male. The males always feed the nesting female. With vomit."

"Reminds me of an ex." Her phone buzzed. She read the screen. "Gotta go."

"What about our date?"

She felt sorry for this clueless man, which wasn't something she typically felt in the course of an evening. Except when she was with the ones who were too ashamed to look her in her eyes but still wanted her to go through the motions. She shoved a spoonful of chili into her mouth and licked her lips. "Mmmmm. Yummy. Thank you for this wonderful date." Her face changed as she sensed something. "Did that have onions?"

Shawn nodded. She sighed and pulled out a small bottle of mouthwash from her bag. Took a swig. She walked over to the sink and spit it out before putting on her long coat. Shawn wrung his hands, suddenly getting nervous. "I thought this would last a lot longer."

"That's what they all say. Sorry. I need to hook up with someone."

Shawn stood up. "I could go with you."

"Go with me?"

"It's too early for our date to end. Right?"

"Listen, Shawn, you should go on a date with someone else. Anyone else." Violet started to get the sense that Shawn was like an eager bloodhound and she needed to throw him off her scent.

Shawn looked down. "Did I say something to hurt you? Sometimes I do that and don't realize it."

"What? No, no. It's nothing against you but— "

"You can't date a guy like me. Not the first time I've heard that." Shawn's shoulders slumped. He sat back down, defeated.

Violet's face softened. She wondered what the harm would be in letting him walk with her to her next appointment. She checked the location on her phone. "This isn't too far from here."

Shawn brightened.

CHAPTER 5

AUDITIONS

Violet had visited high rises before but nothing this fancy. This elevator had a bench. She looked around at the tiny mirrors set in between the interweaving vines carved into the dark wood panels along the elevator walls until the doors slid open.

Shawn led the way through the lobby of Ruth's building. Violet peered at the diamond-shaped lamps and the paintings of fountains adorning the walls. The doorman, with a nametag labeled "Douglas," pretended to be busy behind his desk as his eyes followed them toward the door. He was in his sixties, handsome, with thick hair and a crooked but endearing smile. He held up a small box. "A package for your grandma."

"I'll get it on my way back."

"Is she doing okay?"

Shawn nodded.

"She knows you're going out?"

Shawn beamed. "Of course she does. I'm on a date."

Douglas watched Violet closely as he held the door open for them.

They left the apartment, turned, and strolled up Central Park West. It was one of those rare nights when you could see a few stars peeking through the bright yellowish glow of the sky. A few joggers and neighbors walking their dogs passed by them. Shawn couldn't believe the date was lasting this long. He looked over at Violet. "Who are you meeting?"

"Someone for work."

"What do you do?"

"I … do a lot of acting."

"That's great. Would I have seen you in something?"

"Almost. But, no. A lot of auditioning."

"So this is an audition. They happen at night?"

"They happen all the time. But mostly at night."

Shawn continued walking with Violet, trying to figure it all out.

Violet couldn't remember the last time she had a conversation that wasn't laced with innuendos meant to lure the man in as a customer. There was something slow about Shawn but it was refreshing. He was a nice break from her routine.

They walked across 86th Street until Violet found the right brownstone. "Well, I have your number," she told him. She leaned in to give him a hug but he pulled away.

"Sorry. Hugs. I don't ... too much."

"Oh. Okay. I'll see you around then."

She waved goodbye and walked up the steps. She buzzed the intercom while Shawn watched. An impatient male voice crackled through the speaker. "Yeah?"

"It's me," Violet declared as though she was visiting a dear friend. She looked back at Shawn, who waited at the bottom of the steps and faked a smile to him.

The door buzzed. She lingered for a moment in the opening and glanced back at Shawn's gentle face. It was not the kind of face she was used to. Then she sighed, turned, and entered the bowels of the building while Shawn kept an eye on her.

An unshaven homeless man in a stained overcoat and frayed boots picked through the recycle bin in front of the brownstone, looking for bottles. Finding one, he dropped it into the bag on his shoulder and continued on his way.

Violet came out of the door of the brownstone, looking worn. She checked her phone. It was late. She took a swig of her mouthwash, leaned over the stairs, and spit it out. Then she regained her composure and carefully walked down the steps.

"Did you get the part?"

Violet was startled to see Shawn standing at the curb, holding two cups of coffee. "You waited?"

"I wanted to hear how it went."

"Same as always. I just try to get through it."

Shawn handed her a cup of coffee and beamed. "Gegarang coffee. From Indonesia. I know where we can get more."

"I like surprises but—" She looked away from him. "I've got another ... audition."

"You're very popular."

"I can't believe you stuck around."

"Didn't want our night to end. I hardly know you."

She looked into his eyes and couldn't read anything beyond sincerity. He looked away from her but she didn't think it was from shame. She noticed he was dressed much like the tourists who came to town and found her through online ads her pimp posted about her: *Hot N Sexy! Party girl looking to get together. Fun n amazing. Gr8 at massages. Open to whatever. Generous men only.*

They started walking down the street together. "Most people just care about my measurements."

Shawn nodded. "We can start there." He looked her over. "How tall are you?"

His innocence was energizing. "Five-eight."

"What's your favorite cereal?"

"Any sugar cereal my mom wouldn't let me have when I was growing up."

Shawn stretched his neck. "My favorite cereal is Good Friends."

"That's a cereal?"

"It's the only thing I'll eat for breakfast."

She laughed. "You can't eat Good Friends for breakfast."

Shawn's grandpa once said something similar so he knew it was a joke. He laughed.

"I'm going to invent a cereal called Enemies so people can eat their enemies for breakfast," Violet joked.

"You are?"

Violet giggled. "Don't take things so seriously."

"It helps when people explain what they mean."

Violet waved down a taxi. She started to feel like a kitten with her own ball of yarn.

They hopped inside the cab and Violet gave the driver directions to a hotel downtown. She touched up her makeup while they navigated through the traffic. "Tourists," she told Shawn as though he'd understand those would be her next clients.

"What about tourists?" he asked her.

She caught herself. "Oh, nothing."

Shawn waited on a plush couch in the lobby of this hip hotel. The walls were lined with rows and rows of small blue vases, each holding a single red rose. Old typewriters were suspended from the ceiling. He gazed around the room at the different colors.

He focused in on the burnt orange velvet chair next to him until it started to hum. He moved his gaze to the brown in the painting of a bear and could hear a swishing sound. He turned to the lemon colored lamp next to him, which beeped like a horn.

The elevator doors dinged and opened. Violet stepped out and walked through the lobby, breathing a sigh of relief. As soon as she saw Shawn, she perked up. Part of her didn't think he would wait around but she was glad he did. She approached him, noticing he was lost in thought.

He quickly came back to reality. "How'd you do?" he asked.

"I don't think he could tell I was acting. You okay?"

"Just listening. To the colors."

Violet looked at him, puzzled. Shawn thought of telling her about his autism but didn't want the night to end abruptly. "Some of the senses in my brain are mixed up," he explained. "It's called synesthesia. When I look closely at colors, they have sounds." He left out the detail of it being linked to his autism.

She peered closer at him with interest and pointed to a mauve color. "What's that sound like?"

He made a clanging sound. Her nose wrinkled. "Not what I thought."

Violet sensed someone was watching her and noticed Anton, who leaned against the wall next to the hotel entrance. Anton had the barrel ribcage of a linebacker, because he was one in high school. He was shadowy, in his forties, sporting a red athletic suit. "I'll be right back," she whispered to Shawn.

She approached Anton next to the door. He smacked his lips. "Productive night, sweetie?"

"It's been good."

"You didn't text me back."

"I'm going there now."

Anton glanced over to Shawn. "Who's the guy?"

"Just someone being nice to me."

He squeezed her shoulder. "That's my job," he noted with a kiss on her cheek. "Better get a move on." He pressed himself against her and squeezed her arm tightly to remind her who's in charge. His girls needed those reminders when they weren't quick to answer his texts or their cash didn't add up right at the end of the night.

She nodded. "Right."

Satisfied, Anton strutted out the front door. As he walked down the street, he noticed an elderly woman whose face was withered to a collection of lines and angles. She sat on the sidewalk in a stained overcoat, displaying several books she likely found on the street she was hoping to sell. He dropped a fifty-dollar bill into her Styrofoam cup. The woman looked at him with awe. "God bless you."

"Make your own blessings," he returned.

Violet took a moment, then rejoined Shawn.

"Who was that?" he inquired.

Violet picked a piece of lint off her shirt. "My manager." She smiled weakly as she reached into her purse. She opened a case of pills and popped one into her mouth. She caught his look. "Takes the edge off."

"You should try chamomile tea. It also relieves cramps."

Violet laughed, shocked by the remark. "Okaaay."

"It's the glycine and hippurate."

"Um, I'll keep that in mind." She glanced at her phone. "I've got one more audition."

"Great," Shawn told her, ready for their next stop.

They left the hotel together and Violet hoped Anton was nowhere to notice.

CHAPTER 6

WEIRD PLACE TO MEET

Violet and Shawn ran across Columbus Avenue to the entrance of Central Park, dodging a few honking taxis. They stopped beneath the grand golden statue of a general on a horse with a winged angel leading the way. The air was cold and thin and a breeze blew through the trees, glowing orange from the streetlights.

Shawn looked around. "This is a weird place to meet." He didn't know a lot about acting but he was now realizing it wasn't as glamorous as he thought. He knew actors had to go on a lot of auditions to get a part but never imagined how much effort it took or the strange places they had to go. At late times too. He was glad that wasn't his life. He couldn't handle it.

Violet rubbed her hands together to stay warm. "I've gotta do what I'm told."

A husky police officer plodded by them. Violet motioned Shawn to come closer as she watched the officer make his way around the corner. "Never had good luck with cops."

"Sorry about that."

She pointed to the towering globe of the world at the north end of Columbus Circle across the street. "Can you wait for me over there?"

Shawn nodded, wished her luck, and found his way over to that globe. When he was a kid, he used to challenge Colin to a game of seeing who could find the most countries on that globe the fastest. Shawn always won.

He leaned against the gate next to the orb and glanced over to Violet. He watched as a short man who looked impish in a loosely fitting silvery suit approached Violet, his right hand twitching. They chatted for a moment. Then, he took her arm and they walked down one of the shadowy paths. Shawn strained to see how it was going but couldn't get a good view.

Shawn glanced at his watch. Normally, he was long in bed by this hour. He watched the traffic loop around the circle and whizz by him. The streets were crowded with people walking back from shows, going to catch a late movie, or getting some late night exercise. It always surprised Shawn that no matter what time it was, there were always people on the streets. A white plastic bag fluttered to his feet before the wind whipped it across the street.

He studied the park entrance. Tapped his foot. Suddenly, Violet sprinted out of the park. She darted through the oncoming cars and crossed the street.

Shawn stood up, concerned. She grabbed his arm and pulled him along. "There are some things I won't do for a role," she shouted.

They ran down Broadway, toward the subway entrance. "I know where we can go," Shawn assured her.

They hopped on the 1 Train and rode it to 14th Street, where they made their way through the tunnels. Shawn forgot his earplugs. So by the time they exited up the stairs, the sounds were overwhelming to him.

They walked down 8th Avenue and arrived at Think Coffee, where the pressed tin ceiling glowed from the lights along the walls made from Ball preserving jars. A long glass case full of cupcakes, pastries, and sandwiches led to a round staging area where the baristas would make drinks and the kitchen would deliver food.

The café was quiet with students getting in some late night studying while others read or checked their phones. Shawn loved Think Coffee because it was spacious and he could always hide in a corner with his earplugs and shut out the world. He also liked how passionate they were about their coffee and causes. Cheerful signs posted around the café boasted about their fair trade coffee beans and general love of java. Also, Colin worked there and he was speedy about refilling Shawn's Gegarang coffee, his favorite.

Whenever Shawn visited at the end of the day, Colin always had a few colorful stories to share, such as the one about the older man who undressed himself in the bathroom and stood there until a customer opened the door and let out a shriek.

It was Colin's job to tell the man to leave and while he did, a young lady opened the emergency exit on the other side of the coffee shop, thinking that was the bathroom. The alarm blared throughout the café and people couldn't help but laugh while the embarrassed lady hid her face and the crazy man paraded through the tables without any clothes or embarrassment. The drugs numbed that side of him.

The café used to be a shady nightclub before Think took it over. The only reminder of its former days was that very bathroom with its dark mini tiles and large mirrors covered with graffiti. Colin told

Shawn the entire basement used to be crammed with bathrooms but Shawn could never understand why they needed so many places to pee.

Violet excused herself to the graffiti bathroom when they arrived while Shawn filled Colin in on all the details of their date. Colin couldn't understand why she scheduled auditions in the middle of their time together.

When Violet returned, Colin brought them both coffees, dressed in his brown barista apron. He noticed Violet's skimpy outfit concealed inside her long coat that she promptly closed to his view. "Shawn is obsessed with Gegarang coffee." He announced, placing them on the table. "Shawn says you're an actress."

She nodded.

"What kind of actress are you?"

"You know, the basic kind. How long have you two been friends?"

Shawn smiled. "Colin is my brother."

Violet sat up a little straighter and smiled nervously. "Oh. Okay."

Colin leaned a little closer to the table. "A very protective brother."

Violet checked her phone. "Didn't realize it was so late."

"We just got here."

"It's been a long night."

"I want to see you again," Shawn told her and then he looked away, preparing to be let down.

"Yeah, we'll see."

Shawn started tearing his napkin into tiny pieces. Colin had seen this before. "It'll be okay, bro. Let her have some space."

Standing up, Shawn faced Violet. "I really like you."

"You barely know me."

"I know you're five-eight. You like sugary cereal as long as your mom didn't like it, and acting, and muffins, and eating enemies for breakfast, if you could."

Violet's face lit up. She closed her eyes and asked herself what she wanted next. That wasn't something she did very often. "I'll call you," she told him.

"The last time someone told me that, I waited a long time. And my phone never rang."

"I will. I promise."

"Really?"

"Sure. Have a great night," she told him sweetly. She turned to Colin and tried not to say anything to blow his impression of her. "Good to meet you, too."

She noticed Colin's eyes narrow on her as he faintly smiled and said, "Goodbye." As she left the coffee shop, she tried not to think of her next appointment.

The key to making it through her nights was putting her mind somewhere else while she put what she learned in high school drama class to work. "Oh, yeah. That feels so good," she'd cry out while clutching the sheets and thinking about something she saw on television, ways she could redecorate her apartment, or her favorite brownie recipe. 1/2 cup butter, 1-cup sugar, and 2 eggs. "Mmmmmm. Yeah! Yeah!" 1-teaspoon vanilla extract, 1/3 cup cocoa powder, 1/2 cup flour, 1/4 teaspoon baking powder. "Ooooh, you're such a stud. Come on, yeah." Preheat oven to 350. Melt the butter. Stir in sugar, eggs and vanilla. Beat in the rest. "Oooooh. Oooooh. Ooooooh." Bake in oven for 25 minutes.

The final moment would always end with her collapsing onto the bed, imagining she'd jumped out of the pool after an invigorating swim. Sometimes, the john would want to stare into her eyes as though they were experiencing something real. That made her cringe. She'd always stare right back at him while analyzing why his head was shaped the way it was or trying to figure out what he had to eat for dinner, which was often obvious. The pills were the biggest help in getting her through the nights, though its effects seemed to be diminishing.

Back in the coffee shop, Shawn glowed. "That was my longest date yet."

"She doesn't give me a good vibe."

"Really?"

"It's always good to keep your options open."

"My options are running out."

"You know, Grandma has always bugged me to help you find someone. Maybe it's time I did."

"I like Violet."

"I don't think she's the settling down type. I'll help you find the right kind of girl. We'll start with this," Colin said, motioning to Shawn's polo shirt.

"These are better clothes?" Shawn asked Colin as they made their way through the Diesel store on Lexington Avenue. Shawn could never go into a store like this alone. The colors, patterns and loud music would've drowned him before he even made it to the shelf of jeans made to look like they were worn before they were.

Colin combed through the racks of clothes as Shawn trailed him. "I'm telling you, women want you to look like you care about looking good, but not so good they think you're going to compete for counter space in the bathroom."

"I don't like having anything on the counter."

"Say goodbye to the days of looking like Grandma dresses you."

"She's a big help. What's wrong with that?"

"Nothing, if you're five. But most of us don't wear the same thing every day."

"I mix up the colors."

"You dress like a Lego. Time to dress like a man." Colin picked out some more options.

"I'll forget how to match everything up."

Colin groaned. "We'll take pictures. And maybe we can shape up your hair a bit too." Carrying a pile of trendy clothes, Colin motioned him toward the dressing room.

Shawn inspected his reflection in the three adjoining mirrors outside the dressing room, wearing a new ensemble—a dark blue shirt with a white crisscross pattern, jeans with a few worn spots here and there, and a brown leather jacket. He looked good. Handsome, but approachable. As he looked at himself, he thought, *Not bad.*

Colin coiffed Shawn's hair and made him look even more styled. "Well?" Colin asked him.

Shawn smiled. Since Colin moved out of Grandma's apartment shortly after Grandpa's funeral, Shawn rarely saw him outside of the coffee shop. Colin explained his move as being an opportunity for him to live in Bushwick but Shawn overheard

Grandma asking him to live elsewhere before dinner one night. They didn't talk to each other during that entire meal.

Shawn missed having his brother around. Instead of coming home to Colin sneaking friends into their room, he was now interrupting his Grandma's bridge game or one of her tea parties. Her friends always talked in hushed tones until he stepped into the living room. Then the conversation would get louder and involve something about the Bible. Several of those friends had been coming over to check in on Ruth since her trip to the hospital. Too many visitors made Ruth grumpy. Not enough visitors made her even grumpier.

Shawn looked down at the price tags. Colin noticed him wince. "Don't tell me you can't afford it. You never spend money on anything," Colin declared.

Colin directed Shawn to try on different variations. He mixed up the clothing combinations and took pictures of each. Shawn felt like he was posing for a magazine cover.

On their way to the subway, they stopped by Duane Reed, where Colin printed the pictures. He handed them to Shawn. "Tape these next to your closet and just duplicate the looks."

Shawn took the pictures with newfound confidence. That was something he could do.

CHAPTER 7

KEY SOMEONE ELSE

By Sunday, Ruth felt well enough to venture to church, something she did with Shawn every week. She stood in the living room in a vintage dress with her hair done, carrying her coat on her arm.

"Shawn? I know you don't like church starting without us."

Stepping of his room, Shawn walked down the hall, looking snappy in a new ensemble. She eyed his new look but kept her opinion to herself. "Are you feeling okay?" Shawn asked her.

"I checked my levels and I'm fine. New look?"

He nodded. From her expression, he couldn't tell what she thought, which was the case with everyone.

Because facial expressions didn't register with him, he needed people to tell him what they were thinking.

"Did you ever hear back from your date?"

He shook his head. He felt so hopeful when Violet left him. But each day that passed by drained a little more hope out of his heart. Last night, he decided to join a few new dating websites and was waiting on a couple of women to agree to a date.

"I'm sorry about that. You know, sometimes we need a little encouragement so we don't give up on love," Ruth declared.

She placed something small in his hand. Shawn slowly opened his palm to see a sparkling gold engagement ring and a gold wedding band. He marveled at them, as if he had found buried treasure.

"Doesn't feel right for me to wear them anymore. And I know Grandpa would want you to have them."

"Is this because you're dying?"

"No," she told him, irked. "It's for when you find that special someone someday."

"Thanks so much, Grandma."

She instinctively moved in for a hug but then held herself back, knowing better. She opened the door instead.

As they stepped out of the apartment and walked toward the elevator, Ruth thought about how happy his Grandpa Greg would be, if he knew she gave Shawn her rings.

The night before Grandpa fell asleep and didn't wake up, Ruth asked him how he felt. "Handsome," he told her, before he caressed her cheek. Memories of their very first date flooded into her mind. It was a wintry New York evening at Cozy Soup and Burger on 8th Street in the village, where she ordered chili to bring warmth to her bones. The moment Ruth asked Greg to "hand some" salt to her, he looked at her with a twinkle in his eyes and declared, "You called me handsome." She laughed and knew they had a future together.

Ruth and Shawn left the elevator and walked through the lobby, where Douglas, the doorman, hung up his phone. Shawn couldn't take his eyes off the rings. He thought about the day he would slip them onto his wife's finger. Ruth held out her hand to get them back. "I'll put them in your desk when we get home. For safekeeping."

He reluctantly surrendered them.

Douglas motioned to the street. "Your taxi will be here soon."

Ruth nodded to him politely and turned back to Shawn. "Did you ask about her family?" she asked as she tucked the rings inside her purse.

He shook his head.

"Her job?"

"She's an actress."

"What about her church?"

Shawn shifted uncomfortably. He knew that question was coming. "Not yet."

"You've got to read the sell sheet before you buy the house."

"I'm not buying a house. And I don't even know if she'll call me back."

Ruth struggled to put her coat on. Douglas offered to help. "May I?"

Before Ruth could say no, Douglas helped her slip into her coat. "Glad you're doing well," he told her with a wink. His hand brushed hers and she could feel her pulse quicken. Douglas had always been a soothing presence for her since her husband passed away. He was the first to not just offer help but to actually give it. There were so many things around her home Grandpa regularly fixed, often without Ruth even knowing. But allowing Douglas to step in as her handyman made her feel like she was cheating on her husband somehow.

Their fix it dates progressed into secret walking dates. Ruth would describe to Douglas what it was like growing up on the upper west side while Douglas shared stories about childhood in Harlem. If she recognized someone from the building walking by them, Ruth would stiffen and talk to Douglas as though they were reviewing official business for the homeowner's association.

Their first conversation happened when Douglas asked Ruth about the letters she mailed almost daily. They were always handwritten and addressed to different people in Manhattan, but never the same person twice. Ruth confessed she wrote anonymous letters to random people to tell them how much God loves them. "It's my ministry." She told him. She'd have Shawn print out a list of random people from all over the city and she'd work her way down the addresses. She figured she'd find out the results in heaven.

Shawn didn't notice the moment between Ruth and Douglas. The taxi pulled up outside. "We need to get going," Ruth announced.

"Package for you," Douglas told her, handing her a small box. Ruth's eyes flickered with delight for the briefest of moments, then she was back to business as she waited for him to open the door.

The taxi whisked them through the light Sunday morning traffic. They soon arrived at Redeemer Church on West 83rd Street. Ruth and Shawn emerged from the cab in front of the brick building where people flooded in through the open glass doors.

Ruth noticed a group of women standing around near the street corner. They looked like hookers. Or drug addicts. Or both. There was something sad and used about their clothes, their makeup, their skin. She winced and kept Shawn moving toward the doors.

Inside, Shawn sat next to his grandma in one of the front rows. The small choir sang a soulful song from the stage while Shawn gazed at the multi-colored stained glass windows in the shape of a cross hanging low onto the stage, illuminated by lights behind them.

As Shawn gazed closer at the colors, they seemed to come alive to the music. Each color pulsated with the melody and added sweet-sounding layers to the music. He closed his eyes and prayed, *God, please bring me that special someone soon. Before Grandma dies. I'm worried about her and the future. Please find someone soon. It would be nice if it was Violet. Amen.*

Later that week, Colin convinced Shawn to go with him to a lock and key dating mixer at an Irish pub in SoHo. Nervous men in their 20s and 30s mingled throughout the room, trying to match their keys to the locks being held by equally skittish women. They all sipped beers and munched on pretzels.

Shawn wore an ensemble inspired by Colin. He stood across from an overfed but pretty woman in her twenties who had a faint mustache on her lip. Pointing to his own lip, he informed her, "I see them advertised on TV all the time. You can get that lasered right off."

"Didn't think it was that noticeable," she told him with a frown.

"Anyone can see it's a mustache. But you can fix it."

Shawn couldn't tell she looked like she was about to cry. Colin was suddenly next to them. "Excuse my brother. He can be a little blunt sometimes."

"Did I say something hurtful?"

"Try your key, Shawn."

Shawn held up his key while Colin motioned to the woman's padlock. She held it back. "Oh, come on. Let him try," Colin pleaded.

"This lock is closed for business."

Colin looked at her with puppy dog eyes. "Puh-lease."

She clenched her hand over the keyhole.

"It'll take two seconds."

"Key someone else," she demanded, fleeing to the other side of the bar. Shawn looked around, wringing his hands. The lights above the bar glared at him. The noise of the conversations in the room blended together and rose in volume. All he could do was hold his ears shut.

"Just try a few more locks," Colin told him. From the look in Shawn's eyes, he could see this probably wasn't his best idea.

"Can I try?"

Colin turned and was taken aback at seeing Violet standing there, her coat wrapped tightly around her. She jokingly held up her apartment key.

Shawn's face lit up. "You're here!"

"How could I resist your many, many texts?" She looked him over. "Nice look."

Shawn turned excitedly to Colin. "I told her to stop by between her auditions."

Colin nodded, looked back to Violet. "Can I chat with you for a moment?"

Violet nodded and Colin pulled her aside, out of Shawn's earshot. "What's going on?" he asked her.

"Your brother is persistent."

"Do you know he's a high functioning autistic?"

Violet looked back at him, confused. Colin continued, "It's a mental condition. It can be tough for him to form relationships, communicate, read social cues."

Violet snickered, "I might be one too."

"He can be too trusting, too loyal, and when he hurts, he hurts big time. And he doesn't have money. Did you think he did?"

"Why would I think—"

"Are you really an actress?"

Violet's face reddened. She wasn't ready to be grilled like this. "That's why I moved here. To get my big break," she told him sincerely.

"He deserves a nice woman. No offense, but I don't think you're his type."

Violet could feel a deep anger boil inside of her. *How does he know my type? How can he tell I'm not nice?* She was used to overhearing comments made about her in the streets or in the lobby of a hotel but this guy was looking right in her face. She huffed. "The only time people say 'no offense' is when they know they're going to say something offensive."

"I didn't mean—"

"I know what you meant."

Violet looked over at Shawn. The way he looked at her—it was so earnest, it was painful. She wasn't going to let him go. Not that night. Not with his brother breathing down her neck. "Wanna get something to eat, Shawn?" she asked him.

She glided past Colin and took Shawn's arm. He shook her off but she kept walking as though that was perfectly normal. Before they stepped outside, she shot Colin a defiant glance.

CHAPTER 8

A DIFFERENT WAVELENGTH

Shawn and Violet strolled through Washington Square Park. The air was sweet with the smell of honey-roasted peanuts cooking in a stand at the edge of the park. They stopped to listen to a pudgy man with a long mustache who sang a folk song and strummed his guitar. Shawn dropped a few dollars into his open guitar case.

They ventured down MacDougal Street, past La Lanterna café, where Colin used to work. They passed the bright bulbs of the Comedy Cellar and turned onto Bleecker Street. Violet kept waiting for Shawn to say where they were going but he kept glancing at his phone. "Looking for a place to eat?" she finally asked.

Shawn handed her his phone. She looked at the screen, which was filled with pictures of wedding bells and a smiling bride and groom. "What's this?" she asked.

"One of my favorite wedding sites."

Violet cleared her throat. The phone suddenly felt heavy to her. "Oh yeah?"

"It lists what you need to do a year ahead, eight months ahead, all the way down to the big day. With checkboxes. You can see some of my other favorite sites if you swipe your finger."

She swiped across the screen, not sure why she was walking through Greenwich Village with a guy she barely knew, looking at websites about getting ready for your big day. She peered at links to articles about *How to Give the Best, Best Man Speech, Fancy Invites with a Simple Budget,* and *What Wedding Colors Say About You.* Shawn looked at them too, with a look of delight in his eyes.

"I know a guy who put out an ad: wife wanted." Shawn told her.

"Yeah?"

"He got a bunch of replies that said, 'You can have mine.'" Shawn waited for her to laugh. She didn't.

"Is that a joke?" She asked, looking at him sideways.

He nodded. "Colin's better at those. My grandpa was the real jokester in the family."

She handed his phone back to him. "I'm pretty hungry."

He motioned to his phone. "Inspiring, right?"

"I guess."

"I can't eat certain textures," he told her. "Or casein, which is in milk and cheese or gluten, which is part of wheat. What about something near your place?"

Exactly what she didn't want to hear. "Too far. East New York."

"I like riding the trains. Especially the empty cars. What's your address? I'll look it up."

She hesitated. "1600 Pennsylvania Avenue."

He beamed. "Like the White House."

She nodded.

"Do you have a rose garden?"

Violet laughed. "The only thing growing in my part of town is crime."

"Violet!"

She looked across 7th Avenue, where Anton waved her over. "Give me a minute," she told Shawn.

Violet waited for the light to change and crossed the street. "You got me worried, sweetie, when I didn't hear from you," he told her as she approached.

"You didn't have anyone lined up, I thought—"

"Let me do the thinking. Did you get my text?"

She took out her phone and looked at the screen. "Looks like it froze."

"I'll get you a shiny new one if that's what you need. Anything for my honey. You're good for it."

"It works. Just a glitch."

"You with that guy again?"

"He's harmless. Has a mental condition."

Anton leaned forward and Violet braced herself to be hit. Instead, he softly kissed her on her cheek. "Then meet me over by that place near the thing where we went that one time."

Violet nodded. She was never sure which was worse, being hit or kissed. When he hit her, she knew she did something wrong or didn't talk to him respectfully. But when he kissed her, it usually meant she was about to have a busier night than usual or was going to be paired up with someone who would be especially unlikeable. She watched as Anton strutted away, dreading what the night had in store.

Violet waited for an opening in the cars and ran back across the street to Shawn. "Sorry. Thought I was free tonight." She pulled out her pill case. With a trembling hand, she reached for the one thing that made her nights bearable.

"Something's wrong with your hand."

"Nerves, okay?" she said, defensively. Then, she looked down. Felt bad. "Sorry I snapped."

Shawn's face softened. "I could never go on auditions. Or act. For anything. You're very brave."

It was hard for her to grasp that he still believed her story, but he did. And she was grateful. It gave her a chance to be with someone who treated her like everyone else. She was about to lose that feeling of normalcy for the rest of the night. "Can we try the hug again?" She took a step toward him but he stepped back. "What if I hug you gently?"

She tried to put her arms around him but he pulled out of her grasp. She waited for a moment. "Can you give me a hug?"

He looked up. Scooted a little closer to her. Carefully put his arms around her. She had never experienced someone touch her so gently. "You're warm and smell like flowers," he told her, almost without thinking.

"Thanks." She unbuttoned the top of her coat. "What about my teal blouse? How does it sound?"

Shawn gazed at the color. Listened. "Like whispers."

She smiled. "Sorry to cut this short. I'd like to see you again."

"Really?"

She nodded. "I'll have to work on winning over your brother."

"He doesn't see you the way I do," Shawn told her.

"How do you see me?"

He looked into her eyes. "You're a different wavelength."

Violet motioned for him to say more.

"There are colors we can't see. Beauty that's outside our visible spectrum. There's a lot about you that's not visible to me yet. But I can tell it's going to be beautiful."

Violet could feel her eyes well up with tears but she fought them back. She wasn't used to hearing kind words that weren't veiled threats or tools to get her to do something.

She started to embrace him, but stopped, out of consideration. "Since you won't let me, I'll just say it. I wanna hug you, Shawn."

Her words hung there for a moment. Shawn wasn't sure what to do or say.

"And that's not an everyday event for me. I've had a lot more touching than I need." She thought ahead to the next few hours. To the men who would grope her, push her, press into her, suffocate her, treat her like they owned her.

"What does that mean?" he asked, puzzled.

"I need to go."

Violet smiled tenderly as she walked up 7th Avenue and waved goodbye. As she walked away from Shawn, she could feel the dark cloud descend upon her. She was used to that cloud but when she was with Shawn, she could sense it was breaking up and something new and unexpected was beginning to shine through. But now, their time together felt like a distant memory. She descended the steps into the dimly lit subway tunnel to make her way to the men waiting to invade her.

Over the next couple of weeks, Shawn followed Violet to different spots around the city and waited for her to finish her "auditions." Shawn admired her drive to make it but was surprised at the difficulty of her sessions. Sometimes, all she wanted to do was ride with him to the next one without saying a word.

On a Wednesday afternoon, Shawn sat next to the front window at Think Coffee, typing away on his computer while Colin wiped off the table next to him.

"I showed Violet my favorite wedding websites," Shawn revealed to him.

"And she didn't run away screaming?"

Shawn shook his head.

"Grandma called me the other day. Asked me for details. I filled her in. She didn't get a good vibe either."

Ruth had been pressing Shawn for more information and even though he told her everything, she still thought he was hiding something. She told him she was suspicious of Violet and Colin wasn't allaying her fears.

"I finally have a relationship and you're against it."

Colin finished wiping off the table but couldn't hide his agitation. "You're too trusting. That's how you get hurt."

"Are you talking about Amanda?"

"You carried her picture around for years."

Shawn reached into his pocket and pulled out a picture of Amanda. She was positioned at a three-quarter angle to the camera, looking over her right shoulder and wearing a rose colored dress. She was cute and freckled. Eighteen years old with a shock of red hair.

Colin shook his head in disbelief. "You still do."

Shawn returned the picture to its home in his pocket. After Amanda passed away, he promised himself he would always carry her picture with him, so he wouldn't forget her.

"The way Violet dresses," Colin started. "Makes me think she has a past or something,"

"Do they have a past?" Shawn pointed to three slender ladies in skimpy, tight miniskirts who were ordering at the coffee bar, dressed like they were going out to a club.

"Of course they do. They're not your type either. And those auditions at night, what's that about? You think she's really an actress?"

Shawn's face hardened. "At least I'm thinking about my future. You're probably the only barista here with a teaching degree."

"Hey. Ouch."

"You should be doing more with your life."

"And you should ask her more questions. Get to know her. Find out what she actually does."

Shawn groaned. "That's what I've been doing. Just be happy for me." He slid his computer into his bag and left the coffee shop.

Shawn couldn't wrap his mind around how his brother could be so insistent on him finding someone one minute and yet so against it when he finally did.

Colin didn't approve of Amanda at first either. When Shawn started school at Columbia University, he met Amanda during freshman orientation. He couldn't stop listening to her crimson hair. She invited him to an outing at a jazz club but he explained to her how it would be too stifling for him to go.

Instead of joining the others without him, she suggested they take a stroll across the quiet Columbia campus that night and Shawn agreed. He told her about his programming ambitions and she explained how she wanted to bring medical aid to people in poor countries by getting a nursing degree. When he explained his autism, she told him how courageous he was for not letting that hold him back from anything.

Colin was convinced Amanda was dating Shawn as her personal good deed project. So, he invited himself on one of their dates. Amanda smiled warmly when she met Colin and the conversation quickly turned to Colin's area of expertise—coffee. Colin appreciated her penchant for dark roast and liked her immediately. Then he convinced their grandparents to get on board. None of them ever guessed their relationship would've ended so sadly.

CHAPTER 9

EVERYBODY LIES

Shawn joined Violet for an afternoon stroll inside Central Park at 59th Street, near the horse-drawn carriages waiting patiently for willing tourists. They bought hot dogs from a fast-talking, heavyset street vendor and ate them while walking along the outer path that wound through the park. Joggers and bicyclists whizzed by them. The day was overcast and warm. Violet cinched her coat to conceal her 'working' clothes.

Shawn winced as he ate his bun-less hot dog.

"Not a hot dog fan?" Violet asked him.

"It's the way it feels on my tongue. I try not to think about it," he told her. "Why'd you decide to go into acting?"

"It was always a dream. When I moved here, I didn't get a lot of auditions. Then ... my boyfriend showed me how to act."

"What happened to him?"

"Uh. He's my manager now. I borrowed some money from him. He had me do some favors, some acting, to pay him back."

"Colin doesn't think you're an actress."

"What does he know?" she barked back. Then she realized she was overreacting. "Sorry. Is he always that protective?"

"He says my grandma doesn't have a good feeling about us either."

"You're an adult. Seems like you should be able to decide who you spend time with," she said, wondering if he agreed. She didn't get much of a reaction. "You don't need to tell them everything about us," she added.

"I can't lie. I don't like lies. My grandma says everybody lies but ... it doesn't matter, um, since nobody listens."

"Joke?"

He nodded. "Still trying."

They passed a young couple arguing.

"I'm not saying to lie, just don't tell them all the details so we can see where this goes."

The wind whipped Violet's hair into her hot dog mustard. Shawn grasped her hair and wiped it off with his napkin. Violet was moved by his kindness, by his proximity. It reminded her of a moment in elementary school, when Dwayne Jacobs hit her with a clump of dirt, and Mike Richly defended her. She remembered him brushing the dirt off her hair and then wiping off the tears from her cheek. It was an impressive display of gallantry for a ten year old.

"Every day, my co-workers judge person after person to see which ones should have love. I think the whole reason we exist is so we can be loved," Shawn explained.

"It's a nice thought," Violet returned flatly.

"That's why God created us." He wanted to say more but remembered that when he did in the past, some people nodded in agreement but others would say something sarcastic and explain how he doesn't know how the world actually works. Still, this was going further than he imagined and he needed to tell her his dating rule. "I can tell you're a loving person. But I don't date just to date."

"What do you mean?"

"If I'm dating someone, I see them as a possible wife. If that changes, I stop dating."

"Have you broken up with a lot of girls over that?"

"I never got this far," he said. "Would you keep dating me if you didn't see us getting married?"

Violet took a moment. She could hear Anton's mocking voice inside her head, telling her he's the only one who would ever have someone used up like her. "I don't think everyone should get married."

Shawn looked up to her. "But you want to get married someday…"

"If it's possible." She looked into his eyes for a moment and he let her. She wondered how he would treat her differently if he knew the truth about her.

She glanced away and dug into her purse. "Almost forgot." She pulled out a black silk bow tie and handed it to him. It was the real kind, not a clip on. Shawn caressed the silky fabric and treated it like it was made of gold. "You like talking about weddings and marriage. I saw this at a store and thought you could use it someday. When someone's colors sound right to you."

"A real bow tie. Thank you." He wrapped it around his neck. Then he reached out and took her hand. He didn't know what to do with it so he released it back to her. "I should get back to work."

"I gotta go too," she told him as her face darkened. "Auditions."

Shawn waved goodbye as he walked away, fiddling with his new tie. He glanced back at her one last time with a smile as he kept walking.

Violet watched him descend the steps into the subway and her gaze wandered. She noticed a middle aged couple, nicely dressed, sitting on a bench nearby, holding each other tightly. As the woman nestled her head against the man's chest, Violet felt an ache deep inside her, in a place she didn't like to feel or admit was even there.

When he returned to his desk, Shawn glanced over the pictures of couples taped inside his cubicle. He felt something warm and peaceful inside of him. It seemed only a matter of time before he would have his own smiling picture taped up there too.

Saturday night, Shawn carefully studied one of the pictures Colin took of him in the Diesel store and carefully dressed to match it. Once he successfully mirrored the picture, he knew it was going to be a good night.

He slid a few *You're Pulling My Leg!* cards into the back pocket of his jeans. Then he stuffed snacks into his backpack—chips, gluten-free cookies, and apple juice.

In the living room, Ruth was sitting on the edge of the unforgiving couch, painting a black and white view of Central Park. Shawn pulled a small box out of his backpack as he walked to the front door. "The doorman had this for you. You get a lot of packages."

"Just leave it there." She was starting to think her excuses to walk through the lobby were wearing thin. She needed new reasons to accidentally bump into Douglas. "Big date?"

"I'll be home later," he told her, nervous she was going to ask too many questions.

She dipped her brush into the gray paint on her palette. "Is it with that girl?"

"I need to go."

"How long did it take you to heal from Amanda?"

"Why?"

"When you get hurt, you're like Humpty Dumpty. We can't put you back together again."

That wasn't the first time Ruth compared Shawn to that large egg. He felt almost put back together again except for the ache he felt from Amanda's absence, especially when he saw anyone with red hair or visited a hospital or did something that reminded him of their time together. He edged closer to the door. "It's getting late."

"I'd love her address. So I know where you are."

"I'm an adult. I can make my own decisions."

She gave him a look to remind him he was under her care.

"1600 Pennsylvania Ave."

"Her real address."

"That's it. East New York."

"What's her last name?"

"I ... I don't know."

Ruth's forehead wrinkled with concern. "You're going over to her place and you don't know her last name?" She dipped her brush into the black paint on her palette. "You're smarter than that."

"I'll ask tonight, okay? Why aren't you having friends over for one of your teas?"

"I prefer the tea to hearing about gallstones. At least this makes me feel like I have purpose."

Shawn glanced at her painting. "I liked them better when they were in color."

"Well, this is how life feels now. Without Grandpa." She looked off into the distance as the love birds chirped. "I still remember him telling me how he knew he was ready to retire. He said instead of lying about his age, he was bragging about it."

"Do you have your medical alert bracelet? In case anything happens?" Ruth nodded and motioned to her wrist. She didn't want the wristband at first because it made her feel old and ridiculous, as though she was in one of those commercials where the woman falls and can't get up. But Shawn and Colin didn't let her say "no" and she finally relented.

Shawn made his way out the door and into the chilly evening, on his way to surprise Violet.

CHAPTER 10

HER WORLD

After transferring between two trains and a bus, Shawn was finally making his way down Pennsylvania Avenue. The street was lined with sizable, dull apartments in a rundown part of Brooklyn where Starbucks hadn't yet opened shop.

He approached the entrance to her looming red brick apartment building and scrolled through the names on the directory next to the glass and steel doors. He quickly realized there were too many names to find Violet without her last name. He pulled out his phone and dialed her number. No answer.

"You looking for something, sugar?" a woman asked as she stepped out of the building, picking something from her teeth. Her hair, dense and dark with streaks of snowy white, flowed over her shoulders into a tangled mass that spread across the back of her heavy wool coat. At the center of her smile were two gold teeth.

"I'm looking for Violet."

A smirk spread across her face. She quickly typed a code into the keypad. The door buzzed. "Apartment 2033," she told him with a flutter of her eyelashes. "Have fun."

The elevator was covered with graffiti and it groaned as it ascended. Shawn rode it up to the twentieth floor and made his way down the hallway, past doors where he could hear people fighting, a baby crying, and a TV blaring. He finally found Violet's apartment and knocked. Then he waited.

After he knocked a second time, Violet cracked the door open. She saw it was Shawn and her eyes widened in surprise. Shawn thought something was different about her. Then he realized she wasn't wearing any makeup. She looked clean and pretty.

"Shawn? What are you—"

"You said you like surprises. I thought we could do a movie night."

"How'd you find my place?"

"A woman out front helped me."

"Goldie?"

"She didn't say. You look pretty."

"I do?" She could feel herself tense up. *He's just saying that because he wants me.* But then she remembered he wasn't there as a client.

He pulled a mini red rose plant out of his bag and handed it to her. She took it, touched. "You officially have a rose garden," he announced.

"Now I just need an oval office."

She took a breath and opened her door all the way to welcome him inside.

Shawn entered Violet's narrow studio apartment. A queen-sized bed was against the far wall with a worn-out brown couch nearly blocking its view. A small table and chairs pointed the way to the kitchen at the right of the room and clutter was everywhere. Shawn's look turned to concern. "Did someone ransack your apartment?"

"No, no. I didn't know we were having company."

Shawn noticed a short fence cordoning off an area of the kitchen, where a small brown and white mutt greeted him with a wag of his tail. "Who's this?"

"This little trooper is Barney. I found him on the streets."

Shawn reached out to pet Barney and was met with a flurry of wet licks. He noticed a bandage wrapped around Barney's leg. "What happened to him?"

"A street fight, I think."

"Looks like you're doing a good job taking care of him."

"I do my best."

Shawn suddenly remembered the dream he had the night before. He was placing a rose on top of his grandmother's casket. When the petals touched the coffin, they turned black. He woke up with a start and quietly walked down the hall to his grandmother's room to make sure she was okay.

Ruth didn't appreciate being woken up but Shawn was relieved that she was all right. Violet gave Shawn hope that he wouldn't be alone once his grandmother passed away, which he was convinced would happen any day now.

He noticed several pieces of junk mail on the kitchen table and stacked them in a neat pile. Then he threw out an empty paper towel roll and started to wash the dishes in the sink. Violet fiddled with her necklace. "That's okay, I..." Her voice trailed off as she watched him clean dishes and tidy up. He was organizing and she liked it.

"Why do you live all the way out here?" Shawn asked.

"This is where all the ... actresses stay. It's cheap and our manager likes to keep us together."

"Your manager doesn't have very good taste."

"Tell me about it. Then he keeps most of what I make."

Shawn eyed her, concerned. "Welcome to show biz," she said with a smirk. Whenever Anton gave her a cut of the night's cash, it was only enough for her to cover a few necessities. He explained he needed to keep the rest to cover the cost of taking care of her, protecting her, and paying off a debt she owed him from years ago.

There was a ruckus from the apartment next door. Violet pounded on the wall—thump, thump, thump. "Give it a rest, will you?" She turned back to Shawn. "Sorry about that."

Shawn took one of the *You're Pulling My Leg!* cards out of his pocket and read, "Tell me about an animal you would be if you could."

"What?"

He motioned to the card. "It's from a game. Helps start conversations."

She nodded and thought about it for a moment. "I'd be a tiger with wings. So I could fly off and attack whatever got in my way."

A puzzled look crept across Shawn's face. "It has to be a real animal."

"You didn't say that."

"I'd be a Basilisk Lizard. It can run on top of water."

"You said it has to be real."

"It is real." Shawn insisted as he continued to organize.

Violet noticed he was nearing a bowl of colorful condoms on the end table next to the couch. She walked over, discreetly grabbed it, and hid it under a blanket on her bed.

"What's this?" he asked, picking up an oversized black teddy bear wearing a purple NYU shirt.

"That's Theo. Every week, I stuff ten bucks into him. So one day I can go to acting school at NYU."

"That's gonna take a lot of stuffing."

"Tell me about it. I know it's a stupid dream but Theo keeps me going."

Shawn noticed lingerie hanging in the closet. Violet saw him dart his eyes away. "It's just lingerie," she assured him.

"It gets my heart racing. Like when I walked in on you."

"Nothing wrong with that," she conveyed with a smile.

"There is if you're waiting until you're married to make love," he told her as he shut the closet door.

Violet laughed heartily. Then she realized he wasn't kidding. "You don't have to wait."

"It's the sign that you're bonded and committed to someone for the rest of your life."

Violet twirled her necklace and sauntered toward him in a joking, seductive way. "Or it's a sign that you like to have a good time."

Shawn couldn't understand why she was walking toward him while swaying her hips. "Are you waiting for that special person?"

Violet's thoughts raced to how un-special the men were in her life. There was no waiting with them. They wanted to get down to business fast in whatever way they wanted. Violet always got the sense they were trying to fill up a bottomless pit inside of them, even if it was only for a few fleeting moments.

"Did I hurt your feelings?"

"Why?"

Shawn moved closer to her. "I try to ask that if someone's face changes."

"No, I, um…" She was at a loss for words, not used to someone like Shawn overflowing with innocence and questions. Looking around, she noticed he was starting to get her place in shape. "Can you clean up every week?"

"If I can. Clutter distracts me."

Shawn moved one of her purses to the dresser next to the bed and noticed a small leather-bound journal. He picked it up and flipped through it. Each page had simple painted scenes. One page featured a girl in a park, another of a girl ice skating, and another of a girl crying. Violet took it out of his hands.

"What's that?"

"My diary," she said, tucking it under her arm.

"I didn't see any words."

"I painted what was going on. Made it harder for my mom to get into my business."

He noticed a picture frame poking out from underneath a blue scarf on her dresser. "What's that?" He asked.

Violet pulled out a photo of herself as a little girl with long hair and an innocent smile, riding a pink horse on a carousel. Her parents stood on either side of her. Her mom looked like an older version of Violet but her dad had salt-and-pepper hair and the chest of a weight lifter. "That's me," Violet told him, feeling her face grow warm.

Violet's trip with her parents to Hersheypark in Pennsylvania still had fond memories for her, despite her mom and dad arguing for most of the car trip down. She remembered how her stomach felt fluttery as she thought about visiting Chocolate World, the home of the factory-themed tour ride where she would finally get to see how Reese's Cups and Hershey Bars were made. She heard that the ride ended with an all-you-can-eat chocolate buffet but that turned out to be nothing more than a rumor.

"You're cute. Are those your parents?"

"Before Mom kicked me out."

"Why'd she kick you out?"

"Oh, long story."

"I'd like to hear it."

"Maybe another time."

Shawn noticed another photo on the dresser. This one was of a teenage Violet, peeking out through a wall of hair, standing next to her mom, who looked like she had put on some weight. "You're not smiling as big in this one. Where's your dad?"

"He wasn't with us by then."

"Where was he?"

"He went away," she said, shaking her head, not wanting to go there.

Shawn held up the two photos and asked, "What happened between these two?"

Violet was non-committal. "Something. I don't know. I try not to think about that."

"Why not?"

She reached for her pill box.

"Tell me without taking one of those," he told her.

Violet felt a flash of anger. Who was he, barging in there, asking her all kinds of questions about her life? She pushed her anger down into that place deep inside her and forced a smile onto her face. "It's not a big deal. Things happen. That's life. People do things they shouldn't. Happens all the time."

Shawn didn't let it go. "What did people do?"

Violet could feel her insides start to twist. Her mouth went dry. "It's not like I'm going to see them ever again. Who cares?"

"I care."

Violet looked up as Shawn moved closer to her. She felt raw and exposed and she didn't like it. She vaguely explained what happened as memories flooded into her mind of her parents not believing her when she told them about how a relative touched her. Her mom and dad started to argue a lot more after that and her mom blamed Violet for their marriage issues. Violet didn't mind being the family scapegoat, as long as they stayed together. When her father finally left, she found the courage to stand up to her mother, who soon told her she was no longer welcome in her home.

Shawn carefully put his arms around Violet. But this time, it was his touch that was too much for her. She pulled away and he wasn't sure what to do. "I brought my computer so we could watch movies."

"Your turn to tell me something," Violet insisted.

"I didn't grow up with my parents either."

"They kicked you out?" Violet asked jokingly.

"They weren't doing too well with their marriage and I needed lots of visits with doctors. So my grandparents took us in."

"That was nice of them."

"I almost left them to marry a girl."

"She must've been a special girl"

Shawn hesitated and touched his pocket hiding his picture. "Her name was Amanda. She said she wanted to take care of me for the rest of our lives. But she had a heart condition. Died in college."

"I hope you brought a funny movie. We're gonna need it." Violet said with a wink. Then she realized she needed to be serious. "I'm sorry."

"That's what everyone said when it happened," he told her. Shawn told Violet about when he first got the news about Amanda. No words could help him get over the shock of what happened.

Shawn and Amanda met frequently after their classes to study together. They would work side by side for hours. She knew not to interrupt him when he was deep in a train of thought. Sometimes, he would look up and see her staring at him, smiling. "You're my angel," she told him.

"Angels aren't human," he would remind her and she would always laugh. She knew not to take him too seriously. Sometimes, they would walk back to his grandparent's place and they would talk about the future they could have together. Whenever she visited, Ruth taught her how to handle parts of Shawn's daily routine so she could do it without Ruth's help.

Colin was the one who told Shawn that Amanda was being taken to the hospital after she collapsed in the lobby of her dorm. Shawn stayed by her bedside for a week in the ICU, praying for a miracle that never came.

The day of Amanda's funeral, her mom handed Shawn a notecard with Psalm 40:1 written across it — "I waited patiently for the Lord; He turned to me and heard my cry."

"What's this?" Shawn asked her.

She told Shawn she found it in Amanda's pocket. That was something they did. They wrote down encouraging verses from the Bible and slid them into each other's backpacks or stuck them in places where they'd be discovered the next day. Amanda never had the chance to give this one to Shawn. That verse helped him work through his anger and despair. *He hears my cry. I need to wait patiently on Him,* Shawn told himself.

Shawn turned to Violet. "What takes most people a couple months to get over can take someone like me years."

"Because of the autistic thing?"

Shawn nodded. "Grandma says God gave me a big heart 'cause I'm special but that sounds like a Hallmark card to me. My parents never liked how I didn't get things right away. It was their idea for me to live with my grandparents."

Shawn started to think about his parents, about their awkward phone calls. The last time he and Colin tried to join them for Thanksgiving, they said they had too many other things going on. Why didn't they want us? It was too much for Shawn to keep thinking about. He was about to tell Violet he should go when her phone buzzed. She glanced at the screen.

"Looks like I have plans tonight," Violet told him, disappointed. She gathered some pedicure materials. "Whaddya think? Hot pink or mauve?"

Shawn studied her colorful bottles of nail polish. "I like that one," Shawn said, pointing to a blush red color in her collection. She picked it up. "Yeah. That one. It sounds like a heart beating. Or maybe that's mine."

"You've got good taste."

"You do too. Good night, Violet." He waved to the dog. "Good night, Barney."

Violet talked back to him as the dog. "Good night, Shawn."

Shawn chuckled. He opened the door but then remembered something. "What's your last name?" he inquired.

"Black."

"Your name is two colors."

"You told me black is the absence of color."

"Oh, right." Shawn smiled. "You were listening."

"Thanks for the surprise," Violet told him. "I'm looking forward to our next date."

Shawn brightened. "Me too."

Opening the door, Shawn walked out of Violet's apartment and down the hallway, disappearing from her world.

CHAPTER 11

AS LONG AS THEY HAVE MUFFINS

Shawn typed code into his computer at Exclusively Yours. He glanced at the pictures of brides and grooms taped inside his cubicle. They were all beaming. Content. He couldn't wait to take his own pictures, smiling with the woman who would be by his side for the rest of his life.

He opened his web browser and looked up "How do I get married in New York City?" He read over the details. Marriage license fee. City Hall. No blood test needed.

Tammy passed by his cubicle, wearing a shirt that said "Frack off!" She was handing out party passes "New party?" he asked.

"Jake said you could go this time. Maybe he wants another bet."

She handed him a pass and Shawn looked it over. An art deco style font announced the theme: "Flappers and Gangsters."

"Jake wanted to do Cowboys and Indians, until I reminded him how we raped and pillaged their land."

Shawn returned the invite. "That's okay."

"I don't like glorifying violence either, but he wants all of us to go. You can bring someone."

"We'll see."

Tammy shrugged and continued on her way. Shawn stood up and motioned her back. "I put you through the system to get your history rating."

"History rating?"

"It's a score we're going to launch that evaluates people's pasts so you know more about the person you might want to date."

"Okay."

"You got a low score. Any idea why? Bankruptcies? Anything like that?"

"It's obviously broken," she said curtly.

Shawn turned back to his computer and glanced over his formulas. "It looks good to me." When he looked up, Tammy was gone. She quickly handed out the rest of the passes to the other employees as her heartbeat quickened. She could feel her face getting red.

"Is something wrong?" asked Glen from accounting.

She shook her head but it felt like the air was draining out of the room. She dropped the rest of the passes onto the front desk and made her way down the hallway to the women's restroom. She rushed inside and splashed water on her face. She peered at her reflection.

No one knows, she told herself. *And they never will.* She made plans to take off from work early so she could go visit her favorite vegan bakery.

That night, Shawn sat on an overstuffed red chair in the lobby of the trendy Pearl Hotel on 49th Street. He pulled up a website on his phone—How to Tie a Bow Tie—and practiced. He couldn't quite get it. He was wearing a new ensemble and his hair was styled. He finally had his look down and it suited him.

Ding. The elevator doors opened on the other side of the lobby. Violet wandered out, her pain evident. She popped a pill and her shields slid up.

Shawn noticed her walking over and stuffed the bow tie into his pocket. He smiled. "How was the audition?"

"It didn't go like I thought."

"You'll do better next time." Shawn pulled a piece of paper out of his pocket. "I found some more for you."

"What do you mean?"

"I created an algorithm to search and document auditions for a female in your age range." He handed her the listings. "You probably know about most of those already."

She looked it over. The pages were filled with listing after listing of roles in films, television and on stage. Looking over them reminded her of when she first arrived to Manhattan and eagerly lined up auditions, shaping her day around where they were located. She looked at Shawn with gratitude. "Shawn, thank you. I'd love to be going out for parts like these."

"Just want you to succeed at this."

She looked into his baby blue eyes and started to say something but stopped when the elevator dinged. She noticed a wiry businessman in his forties with a balding head step out of the elevator and adjust his tie. His eyes met Violet's for a moment. Her customer. She could still feel his knee on her back, pushing her into the bed. "I can't breathe," she screamed to him. But he kept going.

Violet couldn't stand to look at him as he approached. She pulled Shawn in for a hug with everything she had. He fought it but she held on until she felt the man push past them. She glanced over Shawn's shoulder to watch him leave through the sliding doors.

She pulled back from Shawn and quickly wiped her tears away, which Shawn didn't notice. It felt like everyone in the lobby was staring at her, even though they weren't.

"Let's not see each other on work nights anymore," she insisted.

"Why not?"

"It's tough making it to all my auditions if I'm always seeing you in between."

"I didn't know that. I'm sorry."

"No, it's fine. My job is demanding."

"You'll get a great role someday," he said with an encouraging smile. Then he pointed to a listing on the piece of paper. "Woman, 20s. Good-looking. Wounded past. Multiple personalities. That could be you."

"I think it is me."

Shawn looked at her, confused.

"A joke," Violet uttered, though she didn't feel like it was. She looked into his eyes again. She could tell he was doing everything he could to not to look away from her. She felt something warm deep inside her, a feeling that he cared for her.

She tenderly caressed his face. He jerked back, then forced himself to let her touch him, if only briefly. Violet wasn't used to touch being such a big deal for someone. Most men in Violet's life couldn't wait to press themselves all over her. She appreciated how Shawn was different.

Violet's phone vibrated. She pulled it out and read the screen. "I'm sorry. My next audition."

"You could skip it."

"My manager would let me have it if I did." She looked into his eyes again and saw how hurt he was. "If I ignore it, he'll find me. I don't know how he does it but he always knows exactly where I am."

"Can I see your phone?"

She handed it to him and watched as he clicked on the screen. "What are you doing?" She asked, getting nervous.

"Turning off your GPS."

He adjusted her settings and handed it back to her.

"That's how he tracked me?"

He nodded. Her phone vibrated again. "You should turn it off."

"He'd know if I did."

"And he'd stop bothering you."

"He'd bother me even more. He gets scary when he's mad."

Violet remembered a year ago, when she ignored Anton's call. By the time he found her, she had never seen him so livid. He backed down when she promised to work even longer on weekend nights. That became her new clock out time ever since.

"What kind of food do you like?"

"Italian."

His face wrinkled with disappointment, since Italian food was all about the gluten. He started to look up restaurants on his phone and discovered one that promised gluten-free options. "I found a place."

She thought through what she could say to Anton. *I was in a bad cell area. I left my phone in the hotel room. I should get a night off now and then.* She smiled as she thought of the look on his face if she told him any of that. Then she thought about how much pain he'd make her feel. He wouldn't kill her, she knew that much. He'd just take her out of commission for a while, until she learned her lesson. She decided not to care. "As long as they have muffins."

They exchanged glances. And laughed.

The cab sped them to an old-world Italian restaurant on Mulberry Street, in the heart of Little Italy. Geranium plants hung from the rafters. Mandolin music played from the single speaker attached to the exposed brick wall next to the busy kitchen.

They shared a tomato and mozzarella appetizer, though Shawn could only eat the tomato. They ate off each other's plates and talked about awkward family moments they wished they could forget.

Then they recalled funny moments they'd seen happen in the city over the years: A woman lying across a tipped over newspaper stand eating a pickle. A mailbox stuffed with fast food trash. Two giant Elmos fighting in Times Square. A couple making out in a dumpster. A man with a sign around his head that read "Tell me off for 25¢." And those few days now and then when the city smelled like maple syrup and no one knew why until they linked it to a factory in New Jersey.

After dinner, they ambled up Broadway and cut across 8th Street, passing a homeless guy with a beard holding a sign reading, "Will polka for pasta," which made no sense to Shawn. Violet gave him a few dollars. They sat on the edge of the fountain in Washington Square Park and listened to a woman play a trumpet in high heels.

Later, they made their way to Magnolia Bakery where they watched the bakers layer thick chocolate frosting onto vanilla cupcakes. Violet devoured a cup of banana pudding while Shawn noshed on a piece of flourless chocolate cake.

Soon after, they walked to the subway station on Waverly Place and stopped on the other side of the turnstile where the tunnels to the downtown and uptown trains forked away from each other. Violet waited for Shawn to give her a kiss or a hug or something but instead he waved goodbye as he continued on toward the uptown train. For the first time in a long time, Violet longed for something more.

CHAPTER 12

SOMETHING UNEXPECTED

Shawn paced around his grandmother's living room, nervous.

Knock. Knock.

He opened the door to see Violet standing there in her long gray coat, clearly trying to cover up her 'work' clothes, though Shawn never noticed. "Where have you been?" he asked her.

"I'm sorry. I got tied up," she explained as she slipped inside. Shawn started to close the door when she stopped him. "Shawn, this is Aleesha and Natasha. They're friends of mine."

Aleesha and Natasha emerged from the hallway. They were both in their early twenties, maybe younger. Aleesha was tall, Jamaican, a little overweight and awkward. She had a plump, happy face and wore a tight shimmery dress and stiletto heels.

Natasha was tall, thin, and Russian. Her hair was straight, her face narrow, and she had dark, intense eyes. She wore a tight lacey red dress and knee-high boots. They glanced around the apartment with wide eyes as they made their way inside. They walked around carefully, as if they were afraid to break something.

Shawn looked at them with dread. "I thought you and I were having dinner."

"I'll share. It's a cold night and they were hungry."

Shawn didn't like when people changed a routine or did something unexpected. He shut the door, locked the security latch and looked through the peephole. Then he started pacing and wringing his hands. Violet could tell something was off. "Everything okay?"

"It wasn't going to be just you and me. I also invited my grandma to join us. It was a surprise for both of you. So you could have time together."

Violet thought about what she was wearing and pulled the opening of her coat tightly closed. "Oh. I love surprises but—"

"She'll be home soon and I don't think she'd like all of you being over."

"Thanks for the warm welcome," Aleesha said snidely.

"I wish you told me," Violet said.

"I didn't want you to get nervous."

"But now I'm super nervous. We have to do that another time."

Shawn noticed Aleesha and Natasha looking around. Aleesha wiped her finger across the bottom of a painting of a tree. Natasha peered into the birdcage at Cloudy and Sunny.

"Are you all actresses?" Shawn asked.

"Yep," Violet said, answering for them. "Same manager."

Aleesha smiled half-heartedly. "One time I had my own Oscar."

"Really?" Shawn asked.

"That was his name."

Violet rolled her eyes. "She's joking."

"Sometimes it's hard to know when people are tellin' the truth," Aleesha added, nodding to Violet.

"We should go, girls," Violet announced.

Shawn held her arm. "Wait."

Violet jerked away from him.

"What's wrong?" he asked.

Violet motioned to her arm. "Just a little sensitive." She forced a smile onto her face and exchanged glances with Aleesha and Natasha. "I'm fine. Can't miss an audition again."

"Did your manager hurt you?"

Violet pulled her coat closed even tighter. "He likes us to be professional. He lost his temper, that's all. It happens now and then. He said he was sorry."

Shawn looked at her with concern. "Doesn't seem right."

Violet shrugged as though it was no big deal. "I'll be okay. Let's come up with a plan for our special dinner."

In her mind, Violet knew that dinner should never happen, just like this relationship shouldn't be happening. She needed to tell him the truth so he could move on with his life and she could return to hers but something kept her from saying anything. Deep inside of her, she wanted to stay with Shawn. He seemed like a light at the end of her long, dark tunnel.

With a click, the top lock on the front door turned and unlocked.

Shawn looked at Violet helplessly.

The front door opened and hit the security lock. Then closed again. Ding dong.

Violet looked between Shawn and the door and snapped into action. She corralled the women down the hallway and into Shawn's bedroom, gently closing the door.

Shawn took a breath. He unlocked the security lock and opened the door to his grandma. She breezed past him, carrying a bag from Zabar's filled with groceries.

"How was the Bible study?" he asked her.

"If more women were like the ones in the Bible, the world would be a much better place," she declared, carrying the groceries over to the counter.

"Oh yeah?" he said, trying to keep her attention away from the hallway.

Inside Shawn's room, the women stood huddled together. They listened to the murmurs of conversation penetrating the walls. They glanced at each other, as though expecting one of them to come up with a plan.

Violet's phone buzzed. She took it out of her pocket and glanced at the screen. It was Anton. Aleesha's phone buzzed next. Then Natasha's. "We've gotta get outta here," Aleesha insisted quietly.

"I know, just give me a second," Violet whispered back. She stepped over to the window and looked through. The cars below looked miniature. They were too far up.

They all looked around the room, searching for an idea. Violet noticed the pictures of outfits taped next to Shawn's closet.

Natasha eyed a few loose dollar bills on his nightstand and discreetly slid them inside the front of her dress.

Aleesha noticed the ant farm on Shawn's desk. She picked it up and softly asked, "What's this?"

"Put it back," Violet demanded.

Aleesha looked through the plastic casing, at the network of tunnels inside. She gasped. "Something's moving!"

In the kitchen, Ruth placed a wedge of aged Gouda cheese into the refrigerator and stuffed the Zabar bag under the sink. They heard a woman yelp.

"What was that?" Ruth asked, turning toward the hallway.

"Would you like to go for a walk?" Shawn asked back.

"I thought you were cooking us dinner."

"I'm not ready yet."

"Don't you need my help?"

"I think I've got it."

"That would be a first. What are you planning on making?"

"Baked meat thing."

"Baked what?"

"I'm forgetting what it's called."

"The last time you tried cooking on your own, I put out the fire."

"I got distracted."

"I'll make sure you don't get distracted again."

"You should leave now," Shawn pleaded with her.

"Don't talk to me like I'm in trouble."

Ruth sniffed the air. "Do I smell bug spray? Or is that perfume?"

Shawn avoided her glance. She looked over at the dining room table. Noticed it was set for three. She looked back to Shawn, suspicious. "Is someone else here?"

Something bumped against the wall. Shawn started rocking back and forth. Ruth looked Shawn in his eyes, trying to figure out what he was hiding. She marched past him and down the hallway. Shawn ran after her but didn't reach her before she opened his bedroom door.

Her mouth opened wide in shock at seeing Aleesha twirling around in her pink bra and panties in the middle of Shawn's room while Violet and Natasha brushed her off.

Ruth covered Shawn's eyes. "What is going on!?!"

Violet gasped and pulled off her coat to cover Aleesha, revealing her own strapless green dress with see-through holes peppered throughout. Ruth's eyes narrowed on her. "Hello again," Violet said sheepishly.

"Why do white people keep ants for pets? That's nuts!" Aleesha yelled.

"She was looking at your ant thing and they got all over," Violet told them before stomping on a few ants with her foot.

Shawn laughed nervously. "Grandma, you remember Violet. My girlfriend. These are her friends, Natasha and Aleesha"

Ruth clenched her teeth. "Don't call someone your girlfriend just because you're spending time with her. This is going to be a major exterminator bill. What are you all doing here?"

"I invited her over."

"We have rules," Ruth declared. "Didn't you say you like rules?" she asked Violet.

"I'm sorry about your ants," Violet said to Shawn.

"My grandpa gave that to me," he told her. "To teach me about productivity."

"That's freaky," Aleesha added.

"Is that your real name, Violet?" Ruth asked, still fuming.

"Of course it is, Grandma," Shawn told her.

"Is it now?" Ruth asked Violet with piercing eyes.

Violet looked down and wrung her hands. "It's more of a stage name. No one uses their actual name. My real name is Olivia."

"Olivia Black. That's pretty," Shawn remarked.

The last time Violet heard someone use her real name was when she was quickly packing what she could into her green backpack, the one she'd been using since elementary school, just after her mother told her she needed to find another place to stay. When she stepped off the Greyhound bus at Port Authority, she also stepped into her new identity.

Violet stomped on another ant.

"I can't wait to discover more about Olivia Black," Ruth said with a strange look of glee.

"That's why I wanted you to have dinner together. So you can learn more about each other. Did I tell you she wants to study acting at NYU?" Shawn asked. He'd been searching NYU's website lately to figure out how much it would cost for her to go there. It was a lot.

"Several times. And I've heard about your family too. They sound very colorful."

"She hasn't seen them in a while," Shawn added.

"That's a shame. Family is important to Shawn. So is your spiritual life. Are you a follower of Christ?"

"Uh, yeah," Violet returned, not entirely sure what she was asking. No one had ever asked her that before but she noticed Shawn brighten at her response.

"Really? What church do you go to?" Ruth asked.

Violet swallowed. "Church of the ... Holy Grail."

Shawn smiled. "Really? That's great. I didn't know."

Ruth folded her arms and sensed a ruse. "Sounds medieval. We should all go to your church this Sunday. That's much better than dinner."

Violet cleared her throat. "Or maybe I could visit your church."

Ruth shook her head. She was enjoying watching Violet squirm. "I want to go to yours. Who's your pastor? Monty Python?"

Shawn beamed. "I'd love Violet to come with us."

Ruth looked her over; Violet could feel her judging eyes. "Fine. But you might want to rethink what you wear."

"She can dress how she wants," Shawn insisted.

Aleesha could feel her own irritation well up inside her. She knew she'd hit that fancy old lady if they stayed much longer. "We gotta go," she announced.

"I'll see you Sunday, Violet," Ruth said, condescendingly.

Aleesha grabbed her dress and they all headed out the door.

Shawn led them to the elevator while Ruth stayed behind to assess the ant damage and search for stragglers.

"I'm so sorry things got crazy back there," Violet told him.

"We'll make up for it on Sunday," Shawn assured her.

"Shoot. I just remembered. I'm—I'm busy Sunday."

"You said you could go."

"I know but I don't belong in a place like that."

"I'm sure it's no different from your church. I'll text you the address."

Aleesha glared at Violet. "This ain't right."

Shawn looked over at her. "What?"

Aleesha locked eyes with Violet. "You should've told him."

"Told me what?"

Violet shook her head. "My real name. I'm sorry. Hardly anyone knows."

"Should I start calling you Olivia?"

"No, still Violet."

"At least you got to talk with my grandma some more."

"Yeah."

The elevator doors opened and the women made their way inside. They pressed themselves against the back wall as the doors slid shut.

Shawn returned to his bedroom, where his grandma was sweeping the floor. "Hiding women in your room. What else are you hiding?"

"Nothing."

Ruth nodded. She knew he didn't lie. But she couldn't shake the feeling he was up to something. "I'm sorry about your ant farm," she told him.

"It's okay."

Ruth took the broom and left his room. Shawn shut the door and leaned against it, thinking. He opened his desk drawer and took out his grandmother's engagement ring. He examined it closely.

He closed his eyes and pictured what Violet was wearing—her green dress with all its holes.

The sound of the green started to fill his mind. It was deep, pulsating. It sounded peaceful. Then, he prayed. *Is she the one?*

CHAPTER 13

THE TOTAL PACKAGE

Shawn busily typed away at his computer inside his cubicle until he noticed Jake towering over him. He pulled out his earplugs. "Do you need something?"

Jake presented Shawn with a black cummerbund.

"What's this?" Shawn asked.

"You like that bow tie a whole lot. Thought you could use something to go with it," Jake told him with a smile.

"Oh. Thank you," Shawn responded, gratefully. He took the cummerbund and wrapped it around his waist.

"Nothing to figure out with that one. So maybe you can spend more time programming and less time practicing being a groom."

"Thanks for thinking about me," Shawn replied with a warm smile. He sat back down in his chair, pulled his bow tie out from his desk drawer and tried to tie it.

Jake winked at Flynn, as though it was all a joke. Then he returned to his office.

Flynn looked over to Shawn, who looked like he was getting ready for prom. He understood why the other employees avoided Shawn; they didn't want to get caught up in a conversation where he dumped a truckload of information on them they only pretended to care about. But he didn't mind as much.

Whenever Shawn talked on and on about something he thought Flynn would find interesting but rarely did, Flynn would use those times to think through his upcoming weekend.

Flynn rolled his chair over to Shawn. "Hey, if you'd like to join the site, I'll let you try again."

"That's okay."

"I think it might be good for you."

"I'm in a relationship."

"Oh? That's great," Flynn responded, not believing him.

Shawn stared off for a moment. "I think she might be the one."

"That's … that's big news," Flynn remarked, swallowing. He looked at Shawn with pity and wondered what was actually going on. He returned to his desk and watched Shawn fidget with his bow tie from the corner of his eye.

Think Coffee was crowded with NYU students in search of a jolt to get themselves through class. Shawn typed away on his laptop in his usual corner spot at the back while Colin took orders behind the counter.

Shawn looked up to see a bookish woman in her forties try to figure out if she should drop her used napkin through the metal slit for recycled paper, the opening shaped like a wad of trash or the opening shaped like a cup.

Colin explained to Shawn how all three went to the same compost pile in New Jersey but the customers didn't feel comfortable when there was only one receptacle; they couldn't believe it all ended up at the same place. So they had to create these different shapes. She decided on the slit.

Then, a tall and lithe woman walked inside, wearing a sleek designer dress. She was in her twenties, with the classic cheeks and hair of a model, because she was one. She gestured, cueing Colin. He seemed to know what it meant. "Ready in a flash," he told her.

"You're the best," she replied.

Colin started his coffee creation in the barista area as she slipped the cashier her credit card.

She soon took a seat at a table next to Shawn, sipped her cappuccino, and crossed her delicate ankles.

Colin snuck over to Shawn's table and sat down, prompting Shawn to take out his earplugs. "Perfect time for you to practice your flirting,"

"Trying to finish up something."

Colin discreetly motioned to the woman. "That's Laura King. She's the total package. She just started coming in. She's a model. Teaches dance on the side." He could see he wasn't hooking Shawn. "Loves colors."

"You should date her."

"I'm the barista."

"But you have a degree. You're just not doing anything with it."

"Would you stop saying that?" Colin didn't like being reminded that he wasn't living up to expectations. Even when they were growing up, his grandparents always seemed to notice the progress Shawn was making but not so much Colin. They probably didn't have enough energy left after helping Shawn. So, Colin started slacking. Then he found quick ways to make himself look good when they did notice. Eventually, he settled with getting by.

Shawn reached into his bag and pulled out some stapled pages. "I downloaded these from the Department of Education website."

Colin read the heading on the first page, "Guide to applying and getting hired." He then dismissively tossed the papers onto the table.

Shawn motioned to his own clothes. "You helped me. Why can't I help you?"

Colin sighed. Not this again. He returned to the counter.

Shawn looked over to Laura. "My brother likes you."

Laura raised her eyebrows and glanced over to Colin who ducked behind the counter.

That Sunday arrived quickly. Ruth waited by the front door of her condo, dressed and ready to go. "Shawn? You wanted to get there early. I don't want to keep your friend waiting."

"Girlfriend!" Shawn yelled from the other room.

"God help us," Ruth muttered to herself. She started to breathe rapidly. She attempted to speak but couldn't. Her body tensed up. Her eyes moved wildly around the room. She headed for a nearby chair next to the sofa and tried to sit but missed the chair. She fell to the floor with a thump.

Shawn heard the noise from his bedroom. "Grandma?" he yelled. No answer. He ran out of his room and down the hall. His eyes widened at seeing her on the floor. "Grandma?"

He rushed over to her. Took her arm. She tried to speak. "It's—It's—"

Shawn took out his phone.

"It's a panic attack. Tell me everything will be okay."

"You're sure it's not the diabetes?"

She nodded. Shawn hung up his phone and helped her off the floor. He took her over to the chair next to the couch. "Everything will be okay, Grandma."

"I need a minute."

"Everything will be okay."

Ruth slowly breathed in and out. In and out.

The lines on Shawn's face deepened with concern. "You're sure it's nothing more? This is how it started with Grandpa."

"You're not helping."

"Everything will be okay. Everything will be okay."

Ruth relaxed into the chair. "I need something to drink."

Shawn went to the sink and poured her some water.

"We never know when our time will come," she told him. Shawn fingered the picture of Amanda inside his pocket.

Within the hour, Ruth and Shawn made their way through the lobby of her condo toward their waiting cab, past a concerned Douglas. "Are you really okay?"

"Still ticking but thanks for asking, Douglas."

He handed Ruth a small package. "This arrived."

Ruth pulled a small, rectangular box from her pocket. "And I found this. I think it's yours."

"Isn't that the pen you bought?" Shawn asked.

Ruth shushed him.

"Thank you, Mrs. Lambent," Douglas said gratefully. Ruth smiled to him. They hadn't been on one of their walks lately and she didn't know how to tell him she missed him without feeling like she was betraying Shawn's grandpa. It was a tricky high wire act.

Shawn fixated on the package in Ruth's lap while the yellow cab travelled up Central Park West. "Can I open it?"

She shook her head.

"Who sends you all those packages?"

"Don't worry about it."

"Please?"

"Fine."

Shawn took the package and carefully opened it, revealing three small tubes of paint in red, yellow, and blue. Ruth smiled. "He knows I haven't painted in color since Grandpa passed away."

"Why is Douglas giving you paint?" Then he realized what was going on. "He's the one sending the packages."

Ruth nodded reluctantly.

"He must like you."

"They're just little gifts, Shawn."

"Why won't you date him?"

"I'm not ... we're not ... don't be absurd. At my age, not acting on love is the closest I will ever come to living out my favorite Jane Austen novel."

"Jane Austen?" Shawn's face went blank.

The cab stopped in front of Redeemer Church. Shawn helped Ruth out of the cab. "Besides, he's a doorman, Shawn," she continued. "How do you think it would look?"

"Why do you care how it looks?"

"You're the one who hid your girlfriend in your bedroom."

Shawn stopped and looked for Violet among the crowd of latecomers entering the church.

Ruth smirked. "As I thought. Like oil to water."

"I told her we'd be here early. Maybe she already left."

"Doubt it."

"She'll show up."

Shawn looked at his watch and fidgeted, wiping his forehead. The morning was not going the way he planned. "Maybe she's inside."

"Her type tends to stay away from the light."

"She hasn't answered my texts."

"It's better this way, sweetie." Ruth held out her arm. He reluctantly took it and they continued into the church.

Violet eyed Shawn and Ruth entering the church from a used bookstore across the street, staying out of their view. She was dressed in a simple blue dress and half her usual makeup. She pretended to peruse the paperbacks outside the bookstore, thinking.

"How much?" a nearby man inquired of her.

Violet jumped. *Am I that obvious?* Her face drained of all its color. "What?" she asked. She turned to face the man who had a deep voice and a muscular build.

"There's no price here," the man informed her, holding up a book.

Violet caught her breath. "Oh. I'm sorry. I don't work here."

She relaxed. Glanced over at the church again. Debated. And started walking across the street.

CHAPTER 14

WHEN COLORS
SOUND RIGHT

Light shined through the stained glass cross hanging on the stage and painted colorful specks across the floor. The musicians played an upbeat song and the congregation sang together.

Violet slipped into the back of the sanctuary and leaned against the wall. She looked over the eclectic crowd and noticed Shawn sitting next to his grandma, in one of the front pews.

"I'm sorry. You can't be here."

Violet looked over to see a tall, sprightly woman with a bobbed haircut trying to escort her away. Violet lowered her head. Waves of shame washed over her—this was no place for the likes of her. "You're right. I'm sorry. I didn't mean to ..."

"We have to keep this area clear for emergencies," the woman stated.

"Oh."

The usher led Violet to a seat in a pew at the back of the auditorium while the congregation sang Amazing Grace.

Amazing Grace, how sweet the sound.
That saved a wretch like me.
I once was lost but now I'm found.
Was blind but now I see.

As Violet watched the musicians lead the singing, a teenager next to her with long, jet-black hair moved closer to share her bulletin. Violet smiled at the gesture of acceptance.

The last time Violet was in church was on a muggy day in New Jersey when the heat clung to her like a wet, warm blanket. She sneaked into a large brick church building a few blocks away from her home and waited outside the door marked "Senior Pastor." She hoped the pastor would return to his office after he was done shaking hands with all the well-dressed people she saw filing out the front doors of the chapel. Hopefully, before her mom noticed she was missing.

But he didn't return to his office before Violet's mom marched down the hallway and gave her a quick slap, reminding her that no twelve-year-old should wander off by herself. When her mom asked what she was doing there, Violet couldn't think of anything to say and didn't talk for the rest of the day.

That was the last time Violet had stepped foot inside a church and the last time she tried to tell anyone else about the way her uncle would lie next to her in her bed and make her do things that made her feel dirty. She thought it was her fault for letting him into her room but didn't feel like she could stop him.

After a while, Violet's body didn't feel like it was hers anymore. Her uncle told her how much he loved her but this needed to be their secret forever. She kept telling herself he would stop and things would get better the next time her parents dropped her off for a visit. But then he'd be back in her bed so she learned to put her thoughts elsewhere until he was finished.

When she finally did tell her parents, they accused Violet of making up stories, especially when her uncle denied all of it. Eventually, her mom told her that no one who makes up stories deserves to live under their roof.

Violet wiped an unexpected tear from her cheek and looked around to see if anyone noticed. She fixed her attention back to the stage and started getting lost in the singing.

Her phone rang. She quickly pulled it out of her pocket and muted it, embarrassed. A few people glanced her way. She checked the screen. It was Anton. *Client waiting. Where r u?* Her shoulders slumped from the weight of it all.

She slowly found the energy to stand up and made her way to the back doors. She took a final look back and Shawn was suddenly next to her, beaming. "I didn't see you. We're up front."

"I got called in."

"On a Sunday?"

"I wish I could say no. I like that song. Feels hopeful."

"It's Amazing Grace."

"It really is."

She walked away but Shawn followed, wringing his hands.

Violet made her way through the outer doors and over to the curb. She waved for a taxi. Shawn caught up to her. "If we were married, you wouldn't have to worry about money, auditions."

She laughed and thought he was joking.

"Is that funny?"

"No, I …"

"Am I someone you would marry?" Shawn asked her while his eyes grew a little wider.

The idea of being hitched to someone for the rest of her life wasn't exactly appealing to her, especially when she thought about how it ended with her own parents. But here was someone who wanted her and could change her future. *But would he want to be with me if he knew what I did?* she wondered. "Shawn, I need to tell you something."

"Yeah?"

"I never thought we'd get this far. Never thought you or anyone else would bring up ... marriage." *How did the conversation turn in this direction?* She couldn't even remember. It felt strange to talk about the 'm' word. She mostly thought of her life in one-hour increments, not in years. Getting through the day was her biggest challenge, she never had time to think about the rest of her life. She laughed again.

"Why do you keep laughing?" Shawn asked her. He was trying to read her face but couldn't. He was starting to feel alone and afraid of what she was going to say.

"There's a lot you don't know about me," Violet started to explain. She could feel her heart beating.

"We can get to know each other as we take care of each other for the rest of our lives," Shawn assured her. He didn't like the direction the conversation was going. He thought she would be thrilled by the idea but instead, she was questioning him. He felt like the ring was burning a hole in his pocket.

"I have a past, well, umm, a present too," Violet told him, stumbling over her words. "I've … I've been with … men before. I didn't wait for marriage."

Shawn looked down. Swallowed. This was hard for him to hear. He always thought he needed to be with someone who wouldn't compare him with someone else she'd been with before. Given that hugs were challenging for him, he wasn't sure how he'd do in the lovemaking department. He dreaded wondering if he was measuring up to the people his wife had been with before him.

He also wanted to be with someone who loved him enough to wait for him. That was important. He knew his grandparents waited and they never had issues in their bedroom; his grandpa confided that to Shawn while they were having an awkward conversation about sex while riding the E train.

Beads of sweat formed on Shawn's forehead. He could feel his breath quicken as he searched for a reply to Violet. His mind wandered to moments in his past he regretted. There were countless times when he treated someone rudely or coldly and didn't realize it until later. Or moments when he was angry and lashed out, especially when he felt pushed into a corner. He lost count of the times when he was too stubborn to apologize.

For years, he refused to say he was sorry to anyone he hurt because that's who he was and people needed to accept him. Colin explained to him he couldn't be that way if he wanted people to like him. It was around that time when his grandparents started bringing him along with them to church.

While he was at church, he learned about how Jesus treated others with kindness, compassion, humility, and grace. And he claimed to be God! He didn't understand why Jesus needed to die on a cross, though.

His grandpa told him that forgiveness always has a cost. He explained to Shawn that if he loaned Shawn his car and Shawn wrecked it, he would forgive him but someone had to pay the cost to restore the car.

Shawn told Grandpa he didn't plan on borrowing a car from God anytime soon but Grandpa told him that our lives are the car; most of us know we've wrecked them to different degrees but from the perfect God's point of view, we've all totaled our life cars. God wants to forgive us but instead of us having to pay the cost for restoration, God paid for it himself, on the cross. Jesus paid for our lives with his own and then became alive again to show he was God and prove that everything he said was true.

It all sounded fantastical to Shawn but when he studied it and read more of the Bible, he felt overwhelmed by the lengths God went through to love and restore him. He liked how the Bible said Shawn could become a child of God. He wanted in on that family.

One of Shawn's favorite Bible verses was when Jesus said, "There's no greater love than to lay down your life for your friends." When Shawn gave his own life over to God, he asked Jesus to forgive him for the choices he made that he knew weren't right. He asked God for a new beginning and a new way to treat people. Maybe this was his chance to be the way he always prayed he could be. And besides, Violet said she's a follower of Christ. So, they're part of the same spiritual family.

He looked up to her, hopeful. "Everyone has a past but God gives us a new beginning. That's what Amazing Grace is all about."

Violet didn't expect that response. She shifted her weight, unsure of what to say. She felt like she needed to turn the conversation back to him. "I've read up on autism but there's a lot I don't know." She had done a few online searches and found a dating site for people with autism, where people wrote about dates that went wrong, ways they could communicate better, and what not to do. She read about people struggling with how to process what came into their brains and how it could often be overwhelming.

"I need help making some decisions, paying bills, reading people's faces, maybe how to dress now and then, but Colin's been a big help there."

"And your family ..." She thought about how they'd react if he ever told them about this idea.

"If we're married, they'll have to accept you." Shawn seemed certain of that.

He pulled the bow tie out of his pocket and quickly wrapped it around his neck. "Violet, I've been waiting my whole life for that special someone."

Violet was taken aback at seeing the bow tie. "You've been carrying that around?"

"For when someone's colors sound right to me."

A yellow taxi pulled up next to them and honked.

Shawn took something else from his pocket and held it out to her. The engagement ring. Violet couldn't believe what was happening. Her heart felt like it was going to leap out of her chest.

He knelt down, looked up at her, and smiled. "Will you marry me, Violet?"

Violet looked over the ring, her mouth was wide open. It was a simple ring. Gold with intricate vines intertwined, bearing a sparkling diamond.

Years ago, she gave up the idea of this moment ever happening in her life. She thought she might get hitched someday if one of her clients wanted her badly enough to pay for her full time, or maybe she would earn extra cash by marrying someone to help them get a green card. But she didn't think she would marry someone who would know about her and still want to be with her. Then again, Shawn didn't know everything about her. If he did, he wouldn't want anything to do with her. She couldn't handle that break up.

She looked to the taxi again and back to Shawn. And that ring. "Marriage didn't work out so well for my parents," she told him.

"We can be different."

"Everyone thinks they'll be different. Maybe we should move in together first." She knew it was a stupid idea and his grandmother would never go for it but she couldn't figure out how to stop the conversation.

"Not until I commit my life to you."

She looked between the taxi and Shawn. If he knew who she was, he wouldn't be on a knee, he'd be pushing her away. "To you, marriage is a big deal. You shouldn't waste it on someone like me."

"Loving someone is never a waste."

Everything seemed to slow down for her. Here was the most loving man she had ever known and he was asking her to marry him. There were parts of him that were different and she didn't understand why but the same was true of her. Except he didn't know what most of those parts were. He can never know.

She stood there for a moment, looking into his eyes. He held her gaze much longer than he normally did. But it started to feel like he was looking into her, into her dark places where no one could look. She couldn't take it anymore. She turned, jumped into the taxi and shut the door. It quickly drove away.

Shawn's mouth dropped open as he watched her go. He felt stunned and crushed. A wave of emotions flooded into his mind. He wiped the tears from his eyes. It didn't feel like they would ever stop.

Inside the taxi, Violet sank into the back seat as they pulled into heavy traffic. "Where do you wanna go?" the driver asked.

"I don't know," she told him. The car got caught in heavy traffic not far from Shawn while the driver waited for her answer.

Horns honked. Folks were yelling. It reminded Violet of the noisy chaos of her apartment building.

And her life. Her forehead wrinkled as she processed this crush of emotions. She needed one of her pills and searched through her purse. She forgot to bring them. When was the last time she forgot them? She debated what was right and wrong inside her mind and it led her to a dark corner of doubt.

She took out her compact to fix her tear-streaked makeup. There he was. In the reflection of her mirror. He rose from the ground and stared after her, wiping his cheeks with his hands. *Do I want Shawn as my husband? Can I make that commitment? I can't even commit to a toothpaste flavor.* She imagined a future without Shawn and it dampened the new feeling of hope she had discovered when they first met. She closed the compact with a snap of finality.

Shawn slowly trudged back toward the entrance of the church. He gazed at the gray color of the sidewalk. The smoky tone started to pulsate to life. It hummed and grew louder and louder until—

A woman's hand tapped Shawn on his shoulder. He turned. Violet stood there, a half smile on her face. She gave him a hungry embrace. Shawn instinctively pulled back. Then he stopped and looked at her. He slowly stretched his arms around her and pulled her in, accepting her embrace.

The noise of the city turned quiet for both of them as they peered into each other's eyes. They felt safe in each other's arms. After a long, life-altering pause, Violet nodded and Shawn beamed.

Shawn slipped back into Ruth's apartment long after she had fallen asleep. He barely slept that night. He kept waking up and glancing at the bride and groom bobbleheads on his desk. Soon that would be him and Violet and he couldn't wait.

CHAPTER 15

LET HER GO

The next day, Shawn's time at work flew by in a blur. He typed in algorithms and asked a few co-workers for various information but he felt like he was floating throughout the day. He took off from work early and rode the subway down to the Office of the City Clerk on Worth Street where he was meeting Violet.

Violet plucked money out of Theo the bear so she could give it to Anton, to convince him she had a client while she was actually off getting married. She swung by a thrift store three blocks from her place and found a lace wedding dress, yellowed but not too badly. She didn't think it was right for her to wear something pure white. She thought if she found a red wedding dress, she'd have to wear that.

Shawn asked her to try to look like the women in the bridal magazines but that was the closest she could get. She looked like a bride from a wedding magazine from twenty years ago.

When Violet ascended the steps toward the Office of the City Clerk, she felt like she was on her way to a costume party, not her own marriage. When Shawn caught sight of her, his eyes welled up. He was dressed in a tan suit with his black cummerbund and bow tie; they weren't tied correctly but were close. "You look ravishing," he told her. "Your dress sounds like humming birds."

"You're not so bad yourself," she returned.

They filled out the paperwork and waited on the benches in the long sterile hallway. The moment finally arrived when their number flashed on a screen above them.

The rotund City Clerk was a man in his forties with short straw colored hair and a look that was either no-nonsense or bored. He sat behind his desk in the dark, wood paneled room and talked them through the ceremony. They finally got to the moment when Shawn slipped the wedding band onto Violet's finger. "I now pronounce you husband and wife."

Leaning forward, Shawn carefully kissed Violet. When their lips touched, it felt like waves of electricity rippled through him, lighting him up with a warm, delicious feeling. It started to feel overpowering but he forced himself to bear it and pulled her in for another kiss. Then another, until the City Clerk muttered, "I've gotta keep this moving."

Shawn and Violet strode down the steps outside, beaming. Everything around him felt magnified and more real. He reached out for her hand. She smiled and gently clasped his. More ripples of energy coursed through him; he didn't want to let her go.

They walked down the sidewalk hand in hand. She looked at the ring on her finger. Then at her watch. "Unzip me? I need to get to my audition," she told him with shaking hands.

"Don't be nervous," he told her as he carefully unzipped her dress. She pulled it off to reveal a blouse and jeans underneath. She stuffed the dress into her large purse.

"Will we still make dinner?" Shawn asked.

Violet nodded. "We've got time."

They took the R train to 8th Street and walked across to 6th Avenue. They arrived at a small brick building sandwiched between a jewelry store and a nail salon. Violet gave Shawn a quick electric kiss, took a swig of her mouthwash and disappeared inside.

Shawn leaned against the building and eyed the traffic passing by. He noticed girls in tutus exit the ballet school across the street and construction workers lining up for an Umami burger next door.

Violet came bouncing out of the building's entrance an hour later. "How'd you do?" Shawn asked.

"He wants me back."

"Wow," Shawn said, proud of his wife.

"He really liked me. Had me do it a bunch of different ways."

"And you did."

"It felt weird at first but then I just went for it."

"Like you always do."

She pulled stapled script pages out of her pocket, her audition script. It was her first real audition in years and she felt good about it. "I have to get these lines down by Thursday," she told him. "I got this one from the list you sent me."

"Really?"

She nodded and gave him a big kiss.

An elegant hostess with flowing blonde hair and long legs sat Ruth and Colin at a corner table in Le Cirque, a classy upper crust restaurant. A sparkling chandelier hung above their table.

"Do you know why Shawn wanted to meet here?" Ruth asked.

Colin shrugged. "Seems fancy for him." He couldn't think of what to say so he tapped his spoon against the table.

Ruth cleared her throat. "We could have easily met at my place. Do you remember where I live?"

"How many times can I apologize for not going to Grandpa's funeral?"

"You went to the Comedy Cellar."

"To honor him. You know Grandpa. He'd tell us he felt like a newborn baby. No hair, no teeth and he just wet himself."

"I don't like when people avoid me."

"I'm not your son."

Ruth clenched her fist. She knew Colin reminded her of a younger version of her son and she tried to not associate the two. "He's not avoiding me. He's avoiding responsibility. Of his sons."

"Shawn and I will always be grateful you took us in."

"Someone needed to look out for your future. Are you ready to look out for Shawn's? He was so close to falling in love with a disaster."

"I am. And you know Grandpa would've taken me to that comedy club."

Ruth shook her head. She didn't want to get into this argument again but they always seemed to.

"When you pass away, I'll go to your favorite museum. It'll be my way of honoring you," Colin reassured her. "The Whitney, right?"

"Depends on what they're showing. Otherwise, MOMA." She smiled a little. "Will you promise to go after my funeral?"

"Promise."

Colin noticed Shawn step into the restaurant, holding Violet's hand, still in his tan suit without his cummerbund or bow tie. Colin motioned to the door and Ruth looked over. Her mouth opened in surprise while Shawn led Violet over to them.

"Grandma, Colin, I'd like you to meet the newest member of our family," Shawn announced while they took to their feet.

Ruth and Colin both stood there, trying to figure out what he meant. Violet smiled uneasily, waiting for them to hug her or shake her hand or something. When they didn't, Violet shrugged, pulled back a chair and sat down. The rest of them silently followed suit.

Colin spoke up. "Uh … what do you mean?"

"We just got married."

Violet proudly showed them her rings. Ruth couldn't believe it. "Tell me you're kidding."

"I'm saving up for a nice honeymoon."

"I told him I don't need that."

"Shawn, is this a joke?" Colin asked.

"You know I'm not good at pretend. I thought Violet could stay at our place now, until we get something on our own,"

"It's not our place. It's mine. And absolutely not," Ruth declared.

Shawn's smile faded. "But she's family now."

"She's a criminal," Ruth returned.

"Why would you say that?"

Ruth continued. "I got the results of her background check and let me tell you, Olivia Black has a rich history. Ask her how many times she's been arrested."

Shawn turned to Violet. "You've been arrested?"

Violet looked down. The room felt like it was closing in on her. "I told you I have a past."

Shawn suddenly burned with anger at his grandma. "What's wrong with you? I finally found the one."

"Don't talk to me that way."

"So did a lot of paying customers before you," Colin added.

"Paying customers?" Shawn asked.

Violet broke her silence. "Stop talking to him like he's a kid."

Ruth's voice raised an octave. "In some ways, he is a kid. Try explaining to him what it's like being arrested for solicitation after you give me back my rings," she demanded, holding out her hand.

"Solicitation?" Shawn asked, confused.

Violet continued. "He's a man with desires and passions and needs like everyone else."

A waiter in his fifties with a long, serious face and precise movements approached the table as Colin faced Violet. "Are you or are you not a prostitute?"

The waiter left quickly.

Violet shrank back from their judging eyes. She could feel shame creeping in from the pit of her stomach. The exhilaration she felt when they exchanged their vows was being crushed under the heavy foot of reality. She peered into Shawn's confused face and searched for something to say. Everything in her said, *Run!* And she did. Away from the table and out the door.

Shawn sat in his seat, stunned. Then he started to go after her.

Colin threw his arms around him. Shawn flailed and tried to push away from him.

"Let her go," Colin whispered to him.

"Violet!" Shawn yelled. Heads turned. Through the window, he watched her rush away from the restaurant and back into her world. "She's my bride," Shawn uttered, not sure what it even meant anymore.

"She's a fraud," Ruth told him. "Running all the way to the nearest pawn shop."

Shawn searched for words. "She told me, she told me—"

"We know what she told you. I told you to be careful and you weren't. You were so obsessed with getting married," Colin told him.

Shawn rocked back and forth and wrung his hands. The room felt like it was spinning. He slammed his fist against the table. People glanced over and whispered to each other.

"We're sorry this happened, Shawn. We thought you left her," Ruth said gently.

Shawn let out a painful moan. The pudgy manager approached to ask them to quiet down but Colin waved him away.

"Why would you do this without talking to us?" Ruth asked. "Marriage is serious business."

"She was going to take care of me. For the rest of my life," Shawn told them.

"Is that why you married her? So she could be your new grandma?" Colin asked.

"I don't know how long Grandma will be around," Shawn declared.

"That's no reason to go out and marry a whore," Ruth stated.

"I ... I was with her at her auditions. She got a call back today."

Colin rolled his eyes. "She got called to someone's bed."

Shawn looked between them. "I don't believe you."

"Shawn, enough. Who do you trust? Her or us?" Ruth asked sternly.

"Think about how many men she's been with, or how many diseases she has," Colin added.

Ruth started to breathe rapidly. She clutched her napkin. "I'm ... having a panic attack."

Shawn stood up. "Just keep telling her everything will be okay."

"Will it?" Ruth asked him with desperate eyes.

Shawn's look said he didn't know. Colin put his arms around Ruth as Shawn sped out of the restaurant and down the street, his mind racing.

The train ride to Violet's side of town was noisy, hot, and crowded. Either the air conditioning was broken or too many people were on the train. He transferred from the F train to the A train to the B83 bus.

When Shawn stepped off the bus, he paced down the sidewalk toward Violet's apartment. The colors around him shouted for his attention. A green neon sign screeched. A yellow streetlight buzzed. A pink sign gave off a metallic scream. The noise was deafening.

Shawn dashed up the stairs to Violet's building and approached the entrance. He stopped to catch his breath. Buzzed her apartment and waited. No answer. Buzzed again. Nothing.

He sat down on the top of the stairs and felt defeated. Then he noticed Violet on the other side of the busy street. She was pacing back and forth with Anton at her side. Aleesha, Natasha and a couple other women stood nearby, waving or calling out to cars zipping by.

Shawn stood up and was about to yell her name when someone pulled up alongside her in a black Lincoln Towne car. Anton squeezed Violet tight to himself and leaned into the car. He seemed to be working out some kind of deal. Then, he opened the door for her. "Violet!" Shawn screamed, running down the steps.

Violet saw Shawn and froze. Startled. Her face showed a flash of regret and then hardened. Anton shoved her into the car.

Shawn bolted across the street and turned to chase after the car. Anton grabbed his arms and pulled him back. "What the hell are you doing?"

"That's ... that's my wife," Shawn stammered.

Anton laughed. "You got the wrong girl, pal."

The car turned the corner down the street and Shawn realized he could never catch it. He hurried down the sidewalk toward the bus stop while fidgeting and squeezing his hands together. Aleesha and Natasha watched him go, feeling sorry for him.

On the bus, he reached into his pocket and took out the picture of Amanda. It was happening all over again.

CHAPTER 16

DAMAGED GOODS

Shawn sat on the edge of the stiff couch in Ruth's living room, his eyes red from tears. His grandma sat next to him. She reached out to rub his back but he pulled away. Colin brought him a glass of water in his favorite cup, the one with zeros and ones on it.

"Violet is damaged goods, bro. Return to sender," Colin declared as he plopped down on the couch next to him.

"We can get it annulled. No one needs to know it ever happened," Ruth assured Shawn.

"At least she was willing to take care of me," Shawn told them.

Colin lightly slapped Shawn across his face. "Come back to reality. That's not why you get married."

Shawn winced from the smack. Physically, he felt like an exposed nerve. His face tensed with pain. Tears streamed down his cheeks. Colin crossed his arms. "I barely touched you."

"He has heightened senses," Ruth reminded him. "Remember in eighth grade when he got punched? He cried for a week."

That incident was forever stuck in Shawn's memory. He was taking the train home from Brooklyn on a Wednesday night and noticed a scrawny thirteen year old with bushy hair and yellow sneakers watching him read his book on superheroes. When Shawn arrived at his grandparent's stop, the yellow sneaker boy followed him and grabbed the book. Shawn held on and asked what he was doing.

The boy tried to yank the book away while Shawn yelled that the book was a gift and belonged to him. The boy punched Shawn in his gut. Shawn doubled over and cried out in a way that frightened the boy. Shawn felt like he was stabbed with a hundred knives.

Colin turned to Shawn. "I'm sorry, bro."

Shawn nodded as Ruth handed him a tissue. He dabbed his tears and could feel his body start to relax again.

"Ever thought of how you'd take care of her?" Colin asked him.

"What do you mean?"

"Sounds like you made it all about you. That's not love, bro."

Shawn felt confused and angry. He looked away from them and at the colorless paintings on the walls. He wished Grandpa was there. He always had nuggets of wisdom at just the right moments or a fun joke if he didn't. One time, he told Shawn, "If you get married, don't let it become a three ring circus." Shawn looked at him, confused. "You know, engagement ring, wedding ring, suffering."

Shawn turned to his brother. "How do you know what love is? You can't even ask that girl out."

"At least I know what love isn't."

"Okay, enough," Ruth piped up. "We can take care of everything tomorrow. It's late."

Shawn slowly made his way into his bedroom and shut his door. He leaned against the desk and took a deep breath. His mind was still racing, processing the whirlwind of events. He noticed the bride and groom bobbleheads on the shelf. He picked them up and examined their fat, happy faces. Then he shoved them into his desk drawer.

He stretched himself across his bed and the tears began to flow. By the time he drifted off to sleep, he'd cried so much, it felt like there were no tears left in him.

That night, he dreamed he was floating on a boat in the ocean. The boat was made out of his grandmother's red velvet coach and water was quickly soaking through it. He yelled to a nearby cruise ship for help. Then he noticed the ship was made out of Popsicle sticks and was on fire. The flames were black and white.

The next morning, Shawn ripped off the cheerful wedding pictures from the walls of his cubicle one by one. It hurt to look at them now. They seemed too happy, too content, too fake. He tossed them into his trashcan and didn't notice Jake approach him. "What's going on with the algorithms?"

Shawn picked up a report from his desk and handed it to him. "It's finished. That's your score."

Jake scanned it. There were a few summary sentences at the top of the page, then a large number two at the bottom. "I'm a two? Is that good?"

"Ten is the best."

"How's that possible?"

"It checks public records, analyzes how often you're mentioned online, number of friends—"

"You did it wrong."

"It's an objective rating of your past. Two out of ten."

Jake glanced around to see if anyone overheard. A few people nearby looked down at their desks. Flynn quickly busied himself at his computer.

Jake crumpled up the piece of paper and threw it into Shawn's trashcan. "This was a complete waste of time."

"I don't think so. People should know what they're getting into."

"No one will want a history score."

"Well, they should."

"Unless you come up with something better, I can't afford to have you around here. I need something that makes our site stand out, not make people feel bad."

Then he leaned in close to Shawn. "And don't ever run me through that program again."

Jake stormed back to his office, passing Tammy.

"What happened to your smiling pics?" she asked Shawn as she approached his desk. Her shirt said "Stop Wars" in the same font style as "Star Wars." Shawn shook his head.

"I thought I found someone," he said blankly. "Turns out she wasn't who I thought she was."

"That happens in every relationship. Everyone hides who they are until they know they'll be loved and accepted. Do you love her?"

"I thought I did."

"Might wanna figure that part out first."

He looked at her blankly.

"Don't ask me how. My love sensor broke years ago."

"What's a love sensor?"

"Forget about it. Just remember the party tonight. We're short on RSVPs so Jake needs everyone there. Make sure you look gangsta," Tammy told him before continuing her rounds.

Shawn nodded. He had forgotten about the party. He used to beg to go to them; now he was dreading it.

Shawn left work early and stopped by Think Coffee to convince Colin to go with him. He noticed Laura sitting a few tables away from the barista bar, looking her normal gorgeous self. She kept glancing over to them but Colin would quickly dart his eyes away.

"Let's make a bet. I think Laura will say 'yes' if you ask her out. She keeps looking at you," Shawn told him.

"That's because you're talking too loud. You didn't even have a best man."

"It was a quick ceremony."

"I always thought you cared about our family."

"I do."

"Then you should've told me what was going on."

"You can help me get the annulment," Shawn said, choking up. He closed his eyes for a moment and collected himself. "Do you want to go to this party with me or not?" He could feel a headache coming on.

Colin groaned. "I can't. I've got an interview tomorrow. Bright and early."

"Interview?"

"For a teaching job."

"Why didn't you tell—"

"Because I hate doing things just because people tell me I should." Colin thought about this. "Maybe I get that from Dad."

"If you hate it so much, why do you tell me what I should do all the time?"

"I'm looking out for you. That's what brothers are for." Colin told him, patting Shawn on his shoulder. "You should go by yourself tonight. You're an adult. Just be careful about who you talk to," Colin said. Then he returned to grinding coffee.

Shawn started to leave but stopped. "How do you know if someone is the one?"

"Well, you shouldn't love someone just because of what she can do for you," Colin said, matter-of-factly.

"But I miss being with her. Talking to her. Her smile. The way she walked."

"If she loved you, she wouldn't have gone back to sleeping with guys, right?"

Shawn nodded. He hadn't thought about that before, but Colin was right. Violet dedicated herself to Shawn for the rest of her life and then the night of their marriage, she left him to be with another man. That was supposed to be their special wedding night. And who knows how many men she's been with since then?

"I'll help you find someone who would never cheat on you. Someone you love so much you can't stand the idea of her being with someone else. She's out there."

"Thanks," Shawn told him. Then he smiled halfheartedly and made his way out the door, on his way to find a costume shop.

A jazz band jammed from the stage set up at the back of the large, airy warehouse. Dressed in a pinstriped suit with a black fedora, Shawn walked past men costumed as gangsters and women dressed as sexy flappers. He glanced around for Tammy or Flynn or someone from the office but he didn't recognize anyone. He felt lost. Uncomfortable. Alone.

The dazzling lights and trumpet sounds started to press in on him.

He noticed Jake at the bar, dressed in a flashy gold gangster suit with a plastic machine gun dangling from his neck. He held court with two women. Then Shawn noticed these weren't just any women, they were Aleesha and Natasha. They were both dressed in short flapper skirts with long beaded necklaces circling their necks.

Jake pointed them toward two men in their twenties who leaned against the other side of the bar, in gangster costumes. The taller one had red hair, a goatee and a belly. The other was thin with black curly hair and broad shoulders. The men looked uncomfortable as they attempted to strike up conversations with different flappers but didn't get any traction.

Aleesha and Natasha nodded to Jake and made their way over to the two men, turning on their smiles. When they approached, the men immediately brightened. Aleesha ran her fingers along the collar of one of them, while Natasha pressed in close to the other. The men savored the attention.

Shawn watched as Aleesha and Natasha laughed and flirted with them. Their conversation seemed so real but Shawn knew it wasn't.

Aleesha whispered something into her man's ear. He nodded and said something to the other guy, who smiled devilishly. They all walked toward the door where people were still streaming in. Their night was obviously just beginning. Shawn followed them, curious to see what would happen next. Before heading out the door, Aleesha stopped and gave Jake a kiss on his cheek. Shawn overheard Jake ask, "Where's Violet?"

"Busy," she informed him.

"Tell her I asked about her," Jake told Aleesha with a wink before he smacked her butt.

Shawn's eyes widened. He felt ill. And angry.

CHAPTER 17

A PRICE TAG ON HER

Shawn buzzed Violet's intercom over and over. Her voice finally crackled through the speaker. "Yeah?" she asked, annoyed.

"It's Shawn. Can I come up?"

A few moments passed before he heard her again. "You can do whatever you want."

Shawn didn't know what she meant by that, but the door buzzed so he opened it and made his way up to her floor.

Shawn banged on her door. Violet cracked it open, pulling a blue bathrobe tightly around herself. She eyed his gangster outfit. "Didn't think I'd see you again."

Shawn couldn't get his words out fast enough. "Why were you at the pimps and hos party? Do you know Jake? My boss, Jake?"

"Relax. Sure. We all do."

"What do you mean?"

"He likes to give his party guests encouragement. Me and the girls are very ... encouraging."

"What does that mean?"

"He fixed it up with Anton for us to spend time with guys at the party. Jake thought we'd fit in with the girls from your site. Jake's not that bad. He tips. Gives us cab fare."

"Have you *been* with him, Violet?"

Shawn squeezed his hands together as he glared at her, shaking. Violet's face stayed hard. "Why do you care? We're over. No more using each other."

"I didn't use you."

"You needed someone to babysit you and I needed a ticket out of here."

Her words stung. The blue of her robe seemed to moan at him. Shawn looked away, ashamed.

Violet reached back inside and handed him the rose plant. "You take care of something for a change."

Shawn took the plant and noticed the leaves falling off the red blooms. "You should've told me what you do."

"So you'd treat me like your grandma does?"

"You told me those were auditions."

"I was with clients."

"You said you got a call back."

"I did. My first. That was real. But this is obviously where I belong."

Shawn wished with all his might he could read her expressions. He heard her words but didn't know if he should believe them. He silently said a quick prayer, *Help*.

He looked into her green eyes. "I miss laughing with you, talking about the day, having a meal—"

"You'll get over me," Violet declared. Then, she slammed the door.

Shawn stood in the hallway, not sure what to do. Here was a woman he connected with, shared his life with, and actually married. And she just shut the door in his face. Shawn felt like he was being dragged under water and he didn't know how much longer he could hold his breath. He wished he had run his algorithms on Violet. If he knew her low score he wouldn't have wasted his time going on dates, laughing with her, finding out about her life…

He started down the hallway but stopped. *If God doesn't hold my past against me, how can I hold it against Violet? Is it about the past or the future?* He returned to her door and spoke softly through it. "Do you miss me?"

"I don't miss any of my clients," she declared from the other side of the door.

"You saw me as a client?"

"A non-paying client. The worst kind."

Shawn's face darkened. All he could do was let out a scream. "Aaaaahhhhh!"

Violet swung her door open. "You wanna get me in trouble?"

"I thought you cared about me. I thought we had a future."

"That's all part of what I do. Maybe you'd have seen that if you weren't so autistic."

Her words felt like a knife plunging into Shawn's heart. His eyes welled up with tears. He noticed her face alter. Her forehead wrinkled and she was blinking a lot. *What does that mean?* "Your face changed," he told her.

Her expression grew tense. "Please leave."

"I got so mad when I thought you'd been with Jake," he confessed to her.

She put her hands on her hips. "Why would you care?"

"He doesn't deserve you. I don't deserve you either. You're not just a replacement for my grandma." He looked her deep in her eyes and endured the intensity. "I love you, Violet."

Her face didn't change. "You're not the first guy to say that."

Shawn nodded. He realized his time there was over and so was their relationship. He started to turn but noticed something peeking out from the bottom of her robe. It was the train of her wedding dress.

He pulled her robe open to see more of the dress and she let him. He slowly slipped the robe off, past her shoulders. It crumpled onto the floor. She stood there, in her yellowing wedding gown. "When's a girl like me going to get a chance to wear a dress like this again?" she said to him with a pained smile.

Shawn noticed she was wearing her wedding rings. He motioned to them. "Did you wear those with your clients?"

Her mouth opened as if she was going to say something. Instead, she turned and retreated into her apartment. Shawn stood there, not sure what to do. Then he followed her inside.

Her apartment still bore the fingerprints of Shawn's organizing. Barney wagged his tail from the kitchen when he saw Shawn. Violet paced around the apartment. "I … I haven't been with any clients since we got married. I told Anton I was sick. He thinks I still am."

Shawn brightened. She faced him and continued. "After the restaurant, I told myself you were my failed escape plan and nothing else. But I've missed the way you see the world, your bad jokes, the way you care about me."

Shawn felt a sense of relief wash over him. She was close enough now for him to feel her breath. He leaned in carefully and gave her a kiss. Barney barked. They both laughed.

Violet pointed to the corners of the room where Shawn could see paper wedding bells and other decorations. "It was going to be a surprise to make our first night special. You know how much I love surprises."

She opened the refrigerator door and pulled out a small two tier white wedding cake. On the top of the cake were two bulldogs dressed as a bride and groom "They ran out of people."

She placed the cake on the dining room table. "I thought we'd come back here, celebrate, grab my things and run away together."

Shawn noticed an ant farm on the kitchen counter and pointed to it. "Thought we could raise ants together," she told him proudly.

She grabbed a fork and took a bite of the cake. "Don't know why I thought my pimp would ever let me go."

"When were you going to tell me about your past?"

"As soon as I knew you really loved me." She stuffed another piece of cake into her mouth. "It's gluten and casein free."

Shawn excitedly took a fork and cut off a piece. He held it out to feed her, as though they were at their wedding. He moved it around, just missing her mouth. She giggled. He finally made it in. She pulled off a clump of cake with her hand. Shawn smiled. She aimed it toward his mouth, smeared some on his nose.

A set of speakers on a shelf in the kitchen caught Shawn's eyes. "Do you have anything nice we could dance to?"

She scrolled through her phone until she found something. "This is called *A Kiss To Build A Dream On.*" She plugged her phone into the speakers. The unhurried, jazzy, Louis Armstrong song filled the room.

Shawn stood up and offered his hand to her. She took it. They held each other closely and swayed to the music. Their first dance.

Barney gazed at them from the kitchen and fought to keep his eyes open. With a yawn, he drifted off to sleep.

The song faded away and Shawn and Violet found themselves yawning. Shawn checked his watch. It was late. Violet reclined across her bed in her wedding dress and beckoned him over.

Shawn could feel his pulse quicken as he followed her to the bed. He stood at the foot of the bed, unsure what to do.

"You'll have to take off your shoes," she told him.

He nodded and quickly kicked them off. Climbing onto the bed next to her, he felt like he was on fire. He let his head sink into the pillow next to her and they gazed into each other's eyes.

She caressed his cheek. His whole body tingled with waves of excitement. What was off limits to him his whole life was now an open door. This was his wife across from him. His actual wife.

He closed his eyes to thank God for this moment. The algorithms he had been working so hard on started parading through his mind. He could see what was wrong with them. Why did he concentrate everything on the past? He started thinking about the origins of the word *algorithm*. Wasn't it named after the Latin translation of a book written by a Persian mathematician, astronomer and geographer? What was his name? That's right, al-Khwarizmi. How long ago was that? The 800s?

Violet studied Shaun, not sure why he closed his eyes or what was going to happen next. Her body felt stiff. Even though she knew they were married, she didn't feel ready for what married couples do on their wedding night. She wondered how sex could ever feel like love for her. Maybe if they had a more official kind of wedding, something that didn't feel rushed? Would that make it feel more real to her?

Shawn's breathing became steady and Violet realized he had drifted off to sleep. Her body relaxed. She scooted closer to him and pressed her head against his warm body. She could feel his chest rise and fall with each breath. It felt comforting. Peaceful.

The sun was up now, washing Violet's apartment with a golden hue. Violet and Shawn dozed in her bed. Him in his pinstriped suit and her in her wedding dress, entwined in each other's arms.

Violet's phone lit up and buzzed on the nightstand next to her. She managed to turn it off without looking at it. Then she wrapped her arms around Shawn and fell back asleep.

The bang, bang, bang on Violet's door woke them up with a start. They could hear Anton on the other side. "Sweetie, I know you're in there."

Violet looked at Shawn, not sure what to do.

"I can't afford you being sick any more. Neither can you," Anton declared aggressively. "I'm breaking this door down in three, two..."

Violet and Shawn exchanged glances. She slid off the bed but Shawn held her back. "It'll be okay," she told him as she walked timidly to the door. She opened it to Anton looming in the doorway, hanging off the top of the doorframe.

"You've got a star client waiting. The big tipper."

"I'm with ... a friend."

Shawn walked over and stood next to her, "Her husband."

Violet glanced at Shawn, happy to hear him announce that.

"You can play house when she's done," Anton told them.

Shawn put his arm around Violet and could feel her body tensing up.

Anton ripped her away from him and shoved her into the hallway. Barney barked. "Shut the hell up!" Anton yelled to the dog before turning to Shawn. "And you. Don't test me."

"She doesn't work for you anymore."

"She's mine until she pays off her debt."

"Her debt?"

Violet looked down, embarrassed. The "debt" started soon after Anton took her in. She met him while looking for cheap Broadway tickets at TKTS in Times Square. Anton was smitten with her and couldn't stop telling her how beautiful she was. He took her to dinner, to a show, got her little gifts for no reason at all. She drank in the attention. No one had ever treated her that way. He soon called her his girl and she called him her lover boy.

They were inseparable and he even paid for her to get an apartment when she couldn't afford one on her own. He made sure her refrigerator was full and she had nice clothes hanging in her closet. His taste was more risqué than hers. He liked to buy her form fitting dresses and fancy high heels she would never buy herself.

Back then, Violet told Anton she felt indebted to him. He told her there was nothing he wouldn't do for her.

On a Saturday when he took her out for breakfast, he talked about his friend Joe. He owed Joe a big favor and thought she could help pay him back. She could be Joe's lover, just for a night. On loan.

Violet hated the idea but Anton insisted it was the only way he could pay Joe back. And not only that, his friend would pay for it. She firmly said "no" and Anton understood. He told her he never should have asked her and would come up with a better plan.

A week later, he proposed his new idea: she would only have dinner with Joe and that would be enough to pay him back. Violet halfheartedly agreed.

Violet met Joe at an upscale hotel in Brooklyn. When she arrived, he offered her some wine to give them time to get to know each other before dinner. He was in his forties, had a jowly face, rough hands and some gray hair that fanned away from his temples.

As she sipped the wine, she felt strange and tingly. Euphoric. Before she knew it, he was on top of her, pressing into her. She yelled out but he muffled her screams with his sweaty hands. She didn't know if she was going to live or die that night. She stopped screaming so she could breathe and she soon blacked out.

She woke up a few hours later on the white tile floor of the bathroom, naked. Her body felt sore all over. She wrapped a towel around herself and limped into the bedroom, where Joe sat on the edge of the bed, talking on the phone. He muted his call and told her to get the hell out.

She sobbed as she grabbed her clothes and quickly got dressed. He pushed her into the hallway and latched the door shut. She called Anton and told him what happened. He picked her up in front of the hotel in his blinged out Range Rover.

Anton felt awful about what happened. He parked the car a block from the hotel and made her wait inside while he went to confront Joe.

When he returned, he told her Joe apologized but he also talked on and on about how good she was with him. Anton opened his palm to reveal the two hundred dollars Joe had given him.

Violet didn't want to hear anything Joe said or see the money. It all sickened her. But it gave Anton an idea. She could pay him back for all he has done for her by going out with more of his friends.

When she refused to meet up with another guy Anton set her up with, he told her he had pictures from Joe of their night together. He'd have to send them to her mom or post them online if she didn't help him out. He asked her if she wanted all her friends from back home to see that side of her. He told her he'd have to do it if she didn't work for him to pay back what she owed.

Violet felt trapped. Confused. Angry. She hadn't worked in awhile and relied on Anton to get by. She didn't have any of her own money. She needed the apartment and all the ways he provided for her. Her mood plunged into despair after she agreed to meet with a few more men. She hated what she was doing.

Anton didn't like seeing her depressed. He gave her some pills to take the edge off and told her he cared about her. He explained that they could make this their business together. He'd take care of her and give her a share of their profits. Violet agreed but only until she could get back on her feet. The pills made it all bearable. But each time she took one, that euphoric feeling seemed to get further and further out of her reach.

When she disagreed with Anton, he would hit her and then apologize, telling her she gave him no other choice and promising he would be different next time. He threatened her and her family until she learned to fall in line.

She kept telling herself this wouldn't last forever, and now and then he'd tell her how close she was to paying off her debt to keep her going. But then something costly would happen. She'd get arrested for solicitation or she'd need to see a doctor. She began to realize the debt she owed would continue to balloon unless she was careful and took better care of herself.

She started cutting back on the drugs. Now she needed a pill only now and then to get through the night or when past memories started to haunt her. She never knew how carefully Anton had calculated each of his moves since the moment they first met.

Now she was finally beginning to see how he had manipulated and groomed her for his own purposes.

"How much?" Shawn asked Anton.

"Too much."

"How much to release her from you?"

"She ain't for sale."

"She has a price tag on her every night. Five thousand?"

Anton's eyes narrowed as he sized up Shawn and thought this through. His wheels started turning. "Ten."

Shawn didn't know where he would get ten thousand dollars. "Then you'll let her go?"

Anton moved in close to Shawn so only he could hear. "You real about this?" Shawn nodded. Anton whispered in his ear. "Then this is between you and me. Anyone else gets involved and you don't see your 'wife' again, or your Central Park West grandma. Got it?"

Shawn felt his body freeze with fear but he nodded. "And she's not with anyone else."

Anton made steeple fingers with his hands. "For fifteen thousand, I'll keep this little money-maker off the streets and under my watchful eye."

Shawn nodded. "Okay."

"See you real soon," Anton told him, with a smirk. Then he pointed Shawn out the door.

As he passed by Violet, she whispered to him, "I love you too."

CHAPTER 18

YOU HAVE TO LEAVE NOW

"Grandma?" Shawn yelled as he dashed into Ruth's apartment. No answer. He looked through all the rooms. There was a new canvas on an easel in her bedroom but no sign of her. He looked at his phone and noticed he had several missed calls from her. He rang her cell but she didn't answer so he left a voicemail.

Shawn paced around the living room, thinking about how intimidating Anton looked, all the money he needed to find, Violet trapped in her apartment. He had a dark feeling he never felt before, as though something terrible was lurking around the corner up ahead. He prayed for God to help him, to work everything out.

He stopped pacing and retreated into his bedroom. Sitting on the edge of his bed, he took the picture of Amanda out of his pocket. He noticed how yellowed and wrinkled the picture had become. He gently kissed it and placed it inside the top of his desk. He said goodbye to her in his heart as he closed the drawer.

He heard the front door open and rushed into the living room. Ruth stepped inside, dressed in a trench coat and a flowery dress.

"Where have you been?" Shawn asked her.

"The cemetery. What about you? I was worried. You never answered your phone."

"Oh no. Grandpa's anniversary. Did you go alone?"

"I went with Colin ... and a friend," she said mysteriously. It was the first time she took Douglas to Greg's tombstone. She usually took those weekly trips by herself, but Ruth thought it was finally time. She was surprised when Colin showed up to accompany her and Colin was equally as surprised when Douglas opened the front door and kept following them through it.

When they reached the gravestone, she told Grandpa about Douglas and some of their dates while Colin listened with wide eyes. By the end of her one-way conversation, Colin was cheering for them. Ruth didn't think it was appropriate for Colin to assert his own opinion to Grandpa but she secretly appreciated it.

"Ready for the annulment?" Ruth asked Shawn.

He swallowed. "We're going to stay together."

"What?"

"I just need to buy her back."

"Buy her back?"

"From her pimp. To pay her debt. Fifteen thousand dollars."

"You don't need to buy an impossible marriage for fifteen thousand. You can get one for free."

"Grandma, I know you have that kind of money. I can do five thousand but that's doing cash advances and giving everything I've got."

"Maybe he'll give you a discount. Does he take coupons?"

"Grandma—"

"I've spent my whole life taking care of you. And when it mattered most, you married in secret. Without bagpipes." She started straightening up the living room.

"Bagpipes?"

"You told your grandpa you'd have bagpipes at your wedding. To honor our heritage."

"I thought she was the one."

"A prostitute? God help you." She picked up a cloth from next to the sink and started to furiously dust the apartment.

"You wanted me to marry someone who's like a woman from the Bible."

"Because you'd be a lot better off."

"Rahab is a woman from the Bible. She was a prostitute. Wasn't she related to Jesus?"

Ruth shook her head in disbelief as she dusted the lamp next to the couch.

"And what about Mary Magdalene? She saw Jesus rise from the dead."

"Please," Ruth said, getting tired of this.

"If Jesus helped prostitutes, why can't you? Is it because you don't want to love anymore?"

"Now you're being mean." She dashed into the kitchen and grabbed the bird feed from the cupboard above the sink.

Shawn followed her over to Cloudy and Sunny who were chirping. "I have never been in love. It is not my way, or my nature and I do not think I ever shall. Jane Austen said that. I looked it up."

"I was joking when I said I wanted to live like one of her novels."

"Well, the joke's on Douglas the doorman. And on my wife. And on your colorless paintings. You said you wanted your life to have purpose. Maybe this is it."

Ruth dropped birdseed into the feeding trough. "You're late for work. And get my rings back. Otherwise, that will be my new life purpose."

After lunch, Shawn stood across from Jake inside his office. A mounted deer head hung above his desk. Pictures of sexy women wearing intelligent looking glasses dotted the walls. A bottle of gin served as a paperweight.

"What if we don't make it about the past but about the future? We can ask people where they see themselves going, who they'd like to be with, what they'd like their future to be all about. Create algorithms based on their answers," Shawn explained.

"I want people looking, not finding. Finding is bad for business."

"This will keep them looking for someone who matches their 'future potential score.' It'll be unique to our site."

"I like it."

Shawn took a moment. "And, I want you to be an abolitionist."

Jake laughed, as he remembered. "We already did that theme and let me tell you, it did not go over so well."

"Not for a party, Jake. For Violet and the other women you've hired for the parties. Those women are being trafficked by their pimps. They're slaves. And you've been a part of that."

"I hired a few performers. What they do in their time is up to them."

"I'm not going to tell the police unless you do it again. But I need you to loan me ten thousand against my future salary so I can buy Violet's freedom."

Jake looked him over. "This sounds more like a threat than a request."

"And you've got a growing business. Maybe you can find a place for them here."

"You already took me for a hundred." He pulls a one hundred dollar bill out of his pocket. "Here's another. For the cause. I just hired entertainers. Nothing more. Now go get to work on 'future potential.'"

Shawn stood there, not sure what to do until Jake waved him toward the door. He returned to his cubicle, defeated. Tammy stopped by, wearing a T-shirt that featured a recycling symbol.

"No more parties for me," Shawn told her.

"No, I overheard. I wanted to tell you I'm proud of you, for standing up to Jake. He's a work in progress but he's coming along."

"You don't know what he's been doing."

"Don't be so sure," Tammy said.

Shawn looked at her, wondering what she meant.

She continued. "The thing is … that's how I first got hired. Then he got me a job here. Took me off the streets."

Shawn looked at her, surprised. Tammy expected him to recoil or make a cruel joke about what she told him. He hadn't been that way before; she just didn't know how her coworkers would respond when they knew the truth. "Thanks for telling me," he told her. Shawn's reaction encouraged her. "I wish he'd help all the women," he continued.

"That's throwing him into the deep end to teach him how to swim."

Shawn's look turned to confusion.

"Never mind," Tammy headed toward Jake's office. "I'll see what I can do. Violet has always been nice to me. Just make sure her diamond is conflict-free."

Shawn watched Tammy go into Jake's office. Then his thoughts turned back to Violet and the thousands of dollars he needed to raise.

As soon as he made the deal with Anton, Shawn started texting Colin to ask for his help. But Colin refused. Shawn thought it might be easier to convince him in person so he took the train to Think Coffee during lunch.

"I told you, I thought it was a terrible idea," Colin declared as he handed a cappuccino to a perky NYU student.

"But if you'll just—"

"Before you say anything else, you know that Gegarang coffee you like so much?"

"Yeah?"

"It's named after the village in Indonesia where we buy the coffee from. My manager told me this morning that our partnership helps them escape being slaves. That's why we buy so much of it. Also because it's earthy, spicy, clean and sweet with a syrupy body—"

"Why are you telling me this?"

"When he told me that, it made me realize I could help rescue someone else who's enslaved." Colin pulled an envelope out of his pocket. "It's two thousand. All I could do."

A smile broke out across Shawn's face. He took the envelope timidly and gave him a hug. "Thanks, brother." Colin's eyes welled up. He couldn't remember the last time Shawn gave him a hug. The two thousand was worth it.

The clouds drank in the rest of the evening light and the sky turned blue-black. Shawn's hopes for collecting Violet's ransom equally dimmed. He took a taxi all the way out to her apartment, without any hope in sight. *Please God, help us,* he prayed.

When he arrived to her apartment, the door was ajar and her place was dark. Shawn turned the overhead light on. "Violet?" He realized she was curled up in bed, buried under a pile of covers, face down.

"The lights. Too bright," she told him, slurring her words, sounding tired.

Her apartment was in disarray and there was no sign of the dog. "Where's Barney?"

"Safe in a new home."

"Why?" Shawn joined her next to the bed and flipped on the lamp. He saw Violet clearly for the first time. Her left eye was purple and swollen. Her face was pale and damp. Her eyes were open but drained of energy.

He was startled. "What happened?"

She pointed to her eye. "A wedding gift. From Anton."

Shawn's anger welled up inside him. He whipped out his phone. "I'm calling the police."

"No, please. The police put girls like me behind bars, not the guys who pimp us. Then Anton would make me pay for that. The other girls too."

He slowly returned his phone to his pocket. That hopeless feeling roared back. "I only have seven thousand."

She looked up to him, genuinely touched. "That's sweet. But he gave you an impossible price to get rid of you. He'd kill me before he let me go. He'll move us to another city any day now."

"Come back to my grandma's home."

"That's the first place he'd look. And I don't think she'll put out her welcome mat."

"My brother's place."

"Girls have tried to get away before. He tracks them down. Then they go missing."

She looked around. Realized her apartment was a mess again. She reached into her purse and pulled out her pillbox.

"You don't need that," Shawn told her, holding out his hand for the case.

"I'm really hurting," Violet pleaded with him.

"We'll get through this together."

She reluctantly handed him her pills. Shawn walked them over to the sink and poured them down the drain. "We should get you to a hospital."

"You should leave before he comes back."

"Not without you."

"As long as he thinks we're with each other, he'll know how to find me. You think I look bad now? I found Barney a new home so he won't hurt him again," she told him, her eyes filling with tears. "You have to leave now, for good."

Shawn shook his head. He reached out and took her hand. She looked into his eyes. And discovered an idea. "Or he'd have to think we'd never see each other again, then he won't look for me at your grandma's place."

"I'm a bad liar."

"It's pretend."

"I'm not good at pretend either."

"It's acting. I'll direct you through it. We'd have to put on a show. Make it convincing. I'll slap you—"

"Too painful."

"I'll pretend to slap you. Pretend."

Shawn gave her a doubtful look and could feel himself sweating.

CHAPTER 19

I KNOW THE FUTURE

Together, they worked on the details of their fight until Shawn told Violet he was ready. They exited her building to debut their show.

Across the street, Anton talked on his cell phone while eyeing his women. Aleesha and Natasha stood on either side of him, waving at oncoming cars and strutting down the sidewalk.

Violet turned to Shawn to make sure he was ready. He nodded to her and gave a thumbs up. They strolled away from the building and toward the steps that emptied onto the sidewalk below. Shawn grabbed Violet's arm and pulled her down the stairs. She yelled so Anton could hear. "I can't go with you!"

"You're mine now!" Shawn screamed back to her, trying not to laugh. It felt so weird for him to say something he didn't mean. He did his best to hide his smile.

"Don't you get it? It was all a lie. You think I care about you? You were just another john."

She pretended to slap him across his face and pushed him away. He played along, his smile breaking through.

"You can't get rid of me. I own you," he told her in his most commanding voice.

"You're crazy. Wake up," she shouted back convincingly. She gave him another fake slap.

"I don't understand."

"Yeah, you do. Now go!"

They were at the bottom of the stairs now, stepping onto the sidewalk. She pretended to knee him in his stomach, just like they rehearsed. He hunched over and let out a fake moan. "I said get lost!" she shouted at him.

Shawn straightened up and looked her deep in her eyes. "I hope I never see you again." He winked at her, happy with their work.

Neither of them realized Anton had darted over to them in the middle of their fight. Shawn was the first to see him right before Anton punched him in his stomach. Shawn doubled over, his body screaming with pain. Anton nailed Shawn with his fist again. A crippling sting ripped through Shawn's body. He collapsed onto the sidewalk. Tears gushed down his face and blurred his vision. "You bothering my sweetie?" Anton yelled.

Violet cringed at the site of Shawn lying helpless on the sidewalk. She spoke with urgency. "I told him to leave. It's over between us. For good."

"You got my 15K pal?" Anton demanded, towering over him.

Shawn shook his head.

"Then it's bye-bye to your babe."

Anton swiftly kicked Shawn in his stomach. Shawn screamed out. His whole body hummed with pain.

"He gets it," Violet told him.

Anton's face filled with rage as he shouted into Shawn's ear. "Do you? Do you get the message?"

Violet stepped forward to hold Anton back but caught Shawn's glance. He painfully shook his head, warning her to stay back as Anton pummeled him. She understood. Shawn was earning her freedom.

"Feels like I'm beating up a kid. You're making me feel bad."

Shawn was desperate for Anton to stop hitting him but he didn't know how to make him stop. With shaking hands, he reached into his pockets and pulled out the hundred dollar bills. Anton grabbed them.

"What's this? A going away present? I'll take it. Now go away."

He gave Shawn a forceful kick to his face. Shawn convulsed. His whole body throbbed. This was a new depth of pain for him. He was woozy and breathing hard.

Anton grabbed Violet and ran his calloused fingers through her hair. "You know I'll protect you no matter what, honey. Now cover up that nasty bruise. I need you in ten."

"I'm too sick to go out. I need to see a doctor or something."

"Are you telling me what you need?"

"No, I ..."

"Ten minutes."

Violet nodded. She ran up the stairs toward her apartment while Anton turned to wave down a cab. Violet glanced back to Shawn, then ran toward the front doors.

A taxi quickly pulled over. Anton opened the back door to the cab and hoisted Shawn onto the backseat. Then he peeled off several bills and handed them to the cabbie.

"Got mugged. He'll be fine. Take him to Central Park West and 72nd."

Shawn could feel his anger welling up inside of him. He turned to Anton and found the energy to blurt out, "I wish I never met her." Anton laughed and slammed the door. The cabbie pulled away.

"You really okay?" the cab driver asked Shawn as he drove them down Pennsylvania Avenue. Shawn could taste blood trickling into his mouth. He couldn't speak.

Violet rushed into her apartment. Slammed the door. How could he hurt Shawn like that? And how could Shawn take it? Her body started shaking uncontrollably. She sobbed. Wiped tears from her eyes.

She looked around. Realized she was taking too long. Anton had her on a short leash. She could never get away from him. Was everything Shawn did for nothing? She folded her hands as she paced. Prayed a desperate prayer. She needed help. She needed a miracle.

She wrote Anton a note: *Went to hospital.*

After stuffing a few items into her large purse, she picked up Theo the bear but realized he was too big. She returned it to the dresser next to her bed. She stuck her hand into its stuffing to search for bills but realized time was running out. Anton could be there any moment. She forced herself out the door.

Rushing down the hallway, she avoided the elevator, in case Anton was already on the hunt for her. She fled down the stairs and arrived at the first floor. She quietly opened the door and peered into the hallway. No sign of Anton. She hurried to the entrance and looked through the glass doors. Still no sign.

She carefully left the building and looked across the street. Anton was busy talking to his girls. Aleesha caught sight of Violet and was about to yell out but Violet frantically shook her head not to. Aleesha got the hint. Instead, she turned back to Anton and kept his attention.

Violet ran down the steps and hugged the wall as she made her way down the sidewalk. She didn't dare look across the street again. She kept walking away from her apartment and her life.

Blocks away, she pulled out her phone and dialed Shawn. "Are you okay?" she asked him.

"Are you?" he immediately asked back. Shawn explained that the cab driver took him to Mount Sinai hospital. She told him she would meet him there and then smashed her phone.

Shawn followed the path of the doctor's penlight with his eyes and was X-rayed, poked and prodded. Violet told him his swollen lips gave him all the benefits of a lip injection without the cost. The doctor assured Shawn his lips would return to normal.

They took a taxi back to Ruth's apartment and successfully avoided questions from Douglas as they made their way to the elevator. Then, they waited for Ruth to return.

An hour later, the door to the apartment opened and Ruth stepped inside, Bible in hand. Then she saw Shawn sitting next to Violet on the couch. They looked like they were both on the losing end of a boxing match. Ruth winced and rushed over to them. "What happened?"

They started to talk but didn't know where to begin. Shawn gave Ruth a wry look. "I wondered what Violet saw in her pimp. Then it hit me."

Violet slowly smiled. "A joke. A well-timed joke."

Shawn and Violet both laughed painfully, unable to stop themselves. Violet turned to Shawn. "Look at the colors on my face. What do you hear?"

"Eeeeeeeeeek." They laughed hysterically. They were losing it.

"Hey, Grandma, I won my wife back after all. How'd I do it? Beats me!"

"And for half price," Violet added. They high-fived each other. But it hurt. They laughed and laughed until the pain and reality returned.

"You've clearly suffered brain damage," Ruth observed.

Their expressions changed from hilarity to horror as their memories washed over them. Their laughing became crying.

Shawn pulled Violet toward him so she could nestle against his chest. As he felt the warmth of her body, Shawn could feel the torment of what happened begin to ebb. Ruth watched them embrace, amazed that Shawn would hold someone that long.

After a moment, Ruth stood up and grabbed a first aid kit from underneath the sink. "We've been to the hospital. We'll be okay," Shawn assured her.

"You don't look okay. Have you told the police?" Ruth asked.

Violet spoke up quickly. "We did everything we could."

Ruth studied Violet with a pinched expression that managed to seem both worried and irritated at the same time. "Shawn, can you go to the bathroom and wet a washcloth?"

"I can do it," Violet said, standing up.

Ruth motioned for Violet to sit back down. Shawn stood up and carefully limped down the hallway, obviously in pain. When he was out of earshot, Ruth leaned close to Violet. "Ten thousand dollars is yours. If you leave my grandson and the city and never come back."

Violet shook her head. Ruth started to breathe rapidly. She could sense an attack coming on. "I heard you want to go to NYU," she said between breaths. "What's their school color? That's right. Violet. Would Violet like to be a violet? You just have to leave my grandson for good." Ruth tried to control her breathing as she waited for Violet to answer.

"I know marriage won't be easy. But we're in it together."

"If anything happens to me, I'll put Shawn into an assisted living facility. They can take care of him."

"We're going to take care of each other."

"You don't have to."

"I want to. That's what you do when you love someone." Violet heard chirping.

Ruth motioned to the covered birdcage in the corner. "You woke up my birds."

"They're not the only love birds here," Violet told her.

"Twenty thousand."

"My husband is priceless." Violet declared, which unexpectedly brought tears to Ruth's eyes. She looked away from Violet and felt her face grow warm.

Violet took a deep breath and slid the rings off her finger. "I know you want these back."

Ruth took back the rings, surprised by the gesture. Her breathing returned to normal.

Shawn returned with the washcloth. "Is it okay for Violet to stay here tonight?"

Ruth looked between Shawn and Violet and stretched the silence until she couldn't lengthen it anymore. "Well, it's your room." Ruth took the wet washcloth and carefully placed it on Violet's forehead.

"Thank you," Violet said to her. She motioned to the easel in the living room. "You prefer oil or acrylic?"

"Oil."

"Me too. Instead of keeping a diary, I used to paint."

"Well, if you can say it in words, there'd be no point to painting," Ruth declared, with a twinkle in her eye.

Shawn put his arm around Violet. Ruth watched them embrace and for the first time, she was okay with it. She gently placed the rings into Violet's hand and retired to her room. Sitting on her bed, she recalled the moment when her husband called her "Priceless." Tears floated on the surface of her eyes.

The next morning, Shawn tried to convince Violet that they should go to the police. Violet agreed to talk to someone at the police station. Nothing more.

Shawn and Violet walked down 82nd Street toward the precinct. They approached the blue doors where a few cops rushed in and out. Violet stopped, looking unsure and nervous. "We should bring them doughnuts."

"It's not like what you think," Shawn reassured her. "I found out they have a whole division for human trafficking."

"I wasn't trafficked. Just paying a debt."

"I think you were. And we were both assaulted."

"I don't feel well," Violet told him, squatting in the middle of the sidewalk.

"There's a number we can text for help. BeFree. It's anonymous."

"I'm free now. We should work on our future, not stay stuck in the past."

"He gave you drugs, right? I'm sure they'll be interested in that too. We should think about the other women's futures."

Violet thought for a moment. "I know the future I want to have."

CHAPTER 20

COLORS AND SOUNDS

The next week, Violet quietly returned to her apartment building. It was a bright morning and she knew Anton was likely sleeping, recovering from the night before.

She carefully opened her door and slipped inside, not sure what would still be there. Everything was exactly how she left it. A mess. She shut the door quietly. Breathed a sigh of relief. She spotted her NYU bear. She grabbed and gave Theo a hug. Then she found her diary and the pictures of her family.

Her door burst open. Anton marched inside, dressed in an athletic suit. He slammed the door behind him. "You snuck back in here? Without even saying hello?"

"You don't own me anymore."

"I own this place. And I've got a backlog of customers who can't wait to get a taste of you."

"I worked for you long enough. I'm moving on with my life now."

"Sweetie, you can retire when you're dead. I've always treated you good. And that's never gonna end." He took a bottle of pills out of his pocket and shook them. "You need a little pick-me-up?"

"You never give me enough pills to get through the night."

"I got whatever you need. You want more? Something stronger? Done."

"What about Aleesha? Natasha? The other girls? What's their debt?"

"They never had it so good. I'm only a daddy who keeps his kids in line."

"We're not your kids."

"I've always treated you like family. Now, you need to get yourself ready to join your sisters. I posted some new classifieds. Demand is gonna be high tonight. Don't mind me, sweetie." Anton pulled out a pocketknife and cleaned under his fingernails.

Violet looked between him and the door. She slowly put the teddy bear onto the bed. "You know why I came back here? To prove to myself that I'm free from you."

"The only thing you proved is how stupid you are."

"I'm smarter than you think, sweetie."

Violet slowly unbuttoned her blouse, revealing a small lapel microphone underneath.

The door swung open. Police streamed into her apartment, guns drawn, shouting for Anton to drop the knife. He stood there for a moment, glaring at Violet. Then he let the knife fall with a thud onto the floor.

A large officer pulled Anton's hands behind his back and kicked the back of his knees, sending him to the floor. He handcuffed Anton, keeping his knee pressed into his back.

The officer pulled Anton up and searched his pockets. He pulled out a small bag of pills and handed it to another officer. Two others joined them to escort Anton down the hallway.

Once he was gone, Violet took a deep breath and embraced Theo.

An officer brought Violet out of the building. Once outside, she saw Shawn who rushed over and wrapped his arms around her.

They held each other as more police officers poured into the apartment building. Anton watched them from the back of a nearby police car, his face taut with anger.

Over the next month, Violet, Aleesha, Natasha and other women who were caught in one of Anton's snares, talked to the investigating detectives. Ruth hired a few lawyers on their behalf but they hardly needed them. Their cases were tried in a courtroom designed for human trafficking victims. Anton and his associates were convicted and sent to Riker's Island.

While the cases were being tried, the women met with counselors and signed up for a rehab program.

Aleesha called her family in Jamaica but didn't tell them all the details about what happened to her. All they knew was that she overstayed her tourist visa but now the government was working out a way for her to stay in the country.

Natasha got in touch with her dad in the city of Nizhny Tagil and told him the job opportunity she thought she was moving there to pursue turned out to be something far worse. They wept together over the phone and he promised to send her money so she could return as soon as possible. She told him she wanted to stay in the United States, to get her life back together. Two other women were brought in but they refused to testify against Anton and left the rehab facility in the middle of the night.

The end of the summer was nearing and the weather began to cool. Shawn and his grandma took their usual trip to Redeemer one Sunday and, once again, Violet told them to go ahead without her. He left his Bible behind and suggested she read the Book of John. He didn't know what else to say.

At church, the jazz quartet led the congregation through "Great Is Thy Faithfulness" set to a contemporary beat.

Shawn was sitting beside Ruth, missing Violet, trying to keep up with the song. He thought about all the prayers he had prayed there, for God to bring him someone special. Someone he could share his life with. Someone he could love. He glanced to the back of the sanctuary and noticed Violet leaving through the rear doors.

When they returned home, Shawn went to his bedroom, which he now shared with Violet. Ruth had bought them a larger bed. Violet changed out the curtains to something more modern and added a few colorful throw pillows.

Theo the bear had a new home on the desk next to the bobbleheads and games. Violet framed some of her diary pages and featured them around the walls. They also started a new ant farm together.

Violet sat on their bed, folding clothes she pulled out of a laundry basket. Shawn gave her a kiss on her cheek. "I saw you at church. Why didn't you sit with us?"

"I can only take parts of it for now. It feels really good but also terrible at the same time. I feel like I'm invisible, yet people see every inch of me."

"Will you sit by me next time?"

Violet looked down. "We'll see."

There was a knock on their door. Shawn opened it to find Ruth standing there. "Would you like to come out for tea?"

Shawn filled with dread. "Your friends only talk about their health problems."

"Not these friends," Ruth assured him, motioning for them to come out.

They followed Ruth into the dining room where Natasha and Aleesha sat at the table, looking wide-eyed, surrounded by teacakes and other treats. "They don't serve tea at the rehab or at that dating site office. At least not proper tea." Ruth told them.

Douglas was there too, looking uncomfortable in a pink serving apron. It was a small price to pay to be closer to Ruth. They were now seeing each other daily and Douglas had joined them for several family dinners. He filled their teacups as Shawn and Violet sat down at the table.

After a few awkward moments of silence, Natasha finally spoke up in her Russian accent. "I finally got me to ze doctor."

"Yeah?" Aleesha asked.

"Got tired of it burning every time I peed," Natasha explained.

Ruth and Shawn exchanged glances. Then Ruth passed around the large plate of teacakes. Shawn looked at his grandma with new appreciation.

Days later, Ruth and Violet sat on a park bench in Central Park, along a path bordered by trees. With their easels in front of them, they both painted from a picture of Shawn and Violet taped to Ruth's easel.

Ruth dipped her brush into the blue paint on her palette and painted in Shawn's eyes. She glanced over to Violet's version. It was rougher, more childlike. Violet caught her looking and laughed at her amateur way of painting. Ruth smiled and reassured her. "It's a rare talent to be able to paint with your heart."

That Sunday, Shawn stepped out of a cab in front of the church. The bruises on his face were healed but he still had a few scratches on his cheek. Ruth came out of the taxi after him, followed by Douglas. Ruth reached out to grasp Douglas's hand. She smiled as they walked by Shawn and entered the church. As a couple.

Shawn was about to step through the doors when he heard Violet yell, "Shawn!" He turned and was surprised to see her walking toward him, in a flowing wine colored dress with small gray polka dots. Aleesha and Natasha were with her. Violet took Shawn's arm and they headed into church with Shawn leading the way.

A month later, billows of clouds dotted the blue sky as Shawn and Violet strolled along Shawn's former favorite dating spot, the High Line. They both looked healthy and healed. They walked next to the babbling stream of water, sharing a cup of sorbet. Violet looked around. "You know what I like about this place? People thought it was worthless until someone realized it just needed a new start."

Shawn smiled, appreciating her. "There's one regret I have," he confessed to her.

"What?"

"Our wedding. It wasn't as special as I always wanted it to be."

She imagined how disappointing that moment must have been for him, after he bookmarked all those wedding websites and came up with a slew of ideas on what would make the perfect ceremony. When she was young, she imagined what that day would be like for her but eventually filed those ideas in a folder labeled: impossible. "And I bet you didn't feel that special either."

"I feel special now," she assured him.

"Not as special as you will," he returned.

"What do you mean?"

As they continued down the path, Aleesha and Natasha approached them, dressed sharply, as though they were going to a dinner party. They started escorting Violet toward the stairs. She looked back to Shawn. "What's going on?"

"You still like surprises?" he asked her.

Violet nodded.

Aleesha and Natasha walked with her down the stairway, to a cab waiting below. "What's going on?" she asked but they didn't say anything. The taxi made its way over to 10th Avenue and pulled up to The High Line Hotel.

Ruth was waiting for them at the curb, dressed in a simple yellow dress. She took Violet's hand to help her out of the taxi. "Please tell me what's going on," Violet implored her. Ruth smiled and motioned for her to follow them into the tall brick building housing the hotel.

They passed through the lobby with its cathedral ceilings, bordered by exposed black beams. They continued down the hallway and exited onto a patio at the side of the building.

The patio was decked out for a fancy party. The tables were covered with white tablecloths with vases of wildflowers at their centers. A couple dozen women were seated at the tables around them but Violet didn't recognize any of them. They smiled happily and clapped at her arrival.

Then Violet saw Tammy who rushed over to her, wearing a pin proclaiming: There is no Planet B. They hugged. "I brought a bunch of women from work," Tammy told her, motioning to the younger women seated around the tables.

"And I filled in the rest," Ruth added, pointing to the older ladies with lived in faces, mixed among them.

"What's all this for?" Violet asked Ruth. She noticed a decorated table against the wall. The centerpiece was a birdcage filled with flowers with a sign above it, "Celebrating the Love Birds." Next to the cage was a tray of meatballs sprinkled with sesame seeds with a sign labeled 'Bird Seed Meatballs.' Sandwiches were named 'Lovebird Sandwiches.' Mini water bottles were labeled 'For Thirsty Birds.'

"You never had your bridal shower," Ruth informed her as she ushered Violet to her seat. The next couple hours were filled with the women giving her advice on marriage and relationships or confessing that things weren't so great in that department for themselves.

Violet kept thinking the party was over until Ruth would announce something else they were going to do.

They competed to be the first to complete a crossword puzzle and all the words were about Violet and Shawn. Aleesha won the game where they had to blindfold themselves and guess cake flavors. Then Tammy suggested Violet open the gifts stacked next to the door. After the first present was fancy pink lingerie, Ruth declared it would be more fun for Violet to open them in private.

As the guests began to trickle out, Violet overheard Tammy talking to Ruth. "What happened to the love birds I made?" she asked her.

"What do you mean?"

"I put them in the cage but they're missing now and the door is open."

"I took them out," Ruth confessed to her. "Because the real lovebirds are finally free."

Violet smiled at the thought.

As Violet said goodbye to the guests, they kept replying "see you soon" until Violet finally asked Ruth why they kept saying that. She motioned for Violet to follow her.

They returned to the lobby with Aleesha and Natasha close behind. They rode the elevator to the fifth floor and Ruth led them down the hallway to one of the rooms.

Inside, a young slender man with wavy hair, wearing a large hoop earring and holding a hair dryer as though he was ready to go into a gunfight, shared a laugh with a petite woman with a handsome face and tanned skin. Ruth cleared her throat and won their attention.

The young man turned to greet Violet. "Are you ready?" he asked her.

"For what?"

The man laughed. "Your wedding."

Violet turned to Ruth, who nodded and handed her a white terry cloth robe and a towel. "Once you're done with your shower, they'll get to work."

Over the next several hours, they fussed over Violet's hair, nails, makeup, and more in a way she had never experienced before.

When the sky pinkened with dusk, Shawn stood ready. He and Colin had spent the afternoon together in Central Park where Colin read passages from books about marriage to him, along with a few verses from the Bible. Shawn especially appreciated hearing, "I waited patiently for the Lord; He turned to me and heard my cry."

Shawn now stood confidently in a classy black tuxedo with his bow tie finally tied perfectly. Colin waited next to him and leaned over. "If you still want free coffee, I'll have to give it to you from the teachers' lounge." Shawn beamed, proud of his brother. "And I asked Laura on a date," Colin continued.

"Really?"

"She said no."

"Don't give up so easily," Shawn encouraged him with a wink.

The air filled with the sounds of a bagpipe playing Amazing Grace. The chords were deep and stirring. The lanky pastor next to Shawn gave him a nod. They were standing in front of a wooden arbor decorated with violets set against a large glass panel overlooking the traffic racing along 8th Avenue below. This was a popular spot for people on the High Line but now it was reserved for only them.

Ruth sat in the front row with Douglas at her side, holding hands. A crowd of friends sat on the wooden benches behind them, including Tammy, Flynn, Ruth's friends and others from Shawn's work. Jake declined his invitation and said he had something else that afternoon. But he actually didn't want to be there as an awkward reminder of Violet's past. Instead, he paid for all the flowers. Anonymously.

Aleesha made her way down the aisle first, grinning as though this was her own special day. Natasha followed her and looked a little nervous. They were both holding bouquets of violets.

Then Violet appeared. She looked stunning in an elegant, flowing white dress. She caught Shawn's eyes and didn't look away. Shawn had never seen her look more ravishing. His mind filled up with her loveliness. Her eyes looked like jewels set against her glowing, joyful face. He could feel his heart racing. It felt like it was just the two of them. He fought to keep the tears down but a few slipped through.

Violet glided down the aisle and took Shawn's hands in hers. They turned to each other as the pastor spoke. "Shawn and Violet—"

"Olivia. It's Olivia," she informed him.

Her face bloomed with a radiant smile. Shawn beamed his own look of delight.

He peered at her billowy white dress. The milky color pulsated with life and blended with the sounds of the vibrant flowers surrounding them to create a beautiful melody in his mind.

Time quickly passed and Shawn and Violet soon found themselves peering into each other's eyes and saying, "I do."

Finally, the moment arrived. Shawn and Violet kissed. It was a tender, romantic kiss that filled their mouths with sweet softness and felt electrifying. The crowd applauded as the Manhattan skyline illuminated around them with all its magnificent colors and sounds.

MAKE A DIFFERENCE

Thank you for reading my book. If you enjoyed *Hooked*, would you please take a moment to leave me a review at your favorite retailer and recommend it to a friend? 10% of proceeds from the sales of *Hooked* are donated to organizations fighting human trafficking so your purchase of this book is having a positive impact on people's lives.

If you or someone you know is caught in human trafficking or you suspect human trafficking, call 1-888-373-7888 or text "help" to BeFree (233733). This toll-free hotline is available to answer calls from anywhere in the United States, 24 hours a day in more than 200 languages.

For additional resources to fight human trafficking, visit WorldOfMorningStar.com/FightTrafficking.

Together, we can make a difference.

All the best,

Allen Wolf

ABOUT THE AUTHOR

Allen Wolf has won multiple awards for his storytelling as a feature film writer, director and producer. The screenplay upon which his first novel, *Hooked*, is based has won numerous accolades. His first feature film, *In My Sleep*, was released worldwide and won multiple film festival awards.

He is also a multiple award-winning board game creator. Allen's games – *You're Pulling My Leg!*, *Slap Wacky*, *JabberJot*, *You're Pulling My Leg! Junior* and *Pet Detectives* – have brought smiles to hundreds of thousands of people around the world.

Allen graduated from New York University's film school where his senior thesis film, *Harlem Grace*, won multiple festival honors and was a finalist for the *Student Academy Awards*.

He married his Persian princess and they are raising their precocious daughter and newborn son. He enjoys traveling around the world and hearing other people's life stories. Allen also cherishes reading to his kids, spending time with his family, chocolate and visiting Disneyland.

See more of Allen's work at WorldOfMorningStar.com.

ABOUT THE SCREENPLAY

The screenplay for *Hooked* won the Screenplay Award at the *Las Vegas Film Festival*, 2nd Place in the *Cinequest Screenwriting Competition*, was a Top 5 Finalist for the *Kairos Screenplay Competition*, Semi-finalist in the *Final Draft Big Break Screenplay Contest*, Quarterfinalist in the *BlueCat Screenplay Competition*, Semi-Finalist for *Table Read My Screenplay*, Quarterfinalist in *Scriptapalooza*, Rated Top 3% of Screenplays at *Script Shark* and won an Honorable Mention at the *Colorado Film Festival*.

To follow or support *Hooked* becoming a movie, sign up at HookedTheMovie.com.

ALSO FROM THE AUTHOR

Allen Wolf wrote, directed and produced the psychological thriller, *In My Sleep*, which won multiple festival awards including *Best Picture* and the *Audience Award*. See more at InMySleep.com.

Savvy Entertainment ... filmmaker Allen Wolf torques this high-concept premise to darkest dimension. Narratively, *In My Sleep* never rests, a credit to the tight, psychologically astute pacing of filmmaker Wolf.

- *The Hollywood Reporter*

Genuinely suspenseful moments.

- *New York Magazine*

In My Sleep is a brilliantly written thriller that genuinely keeps one guessing throughout the movie. The pacing is superb and the performances topnotch. Allen Wolf has created a very well made thriller.

- *Movie Guide*

ALSO FROM THE AUTHOR

Allen Wolf has created five board games that have won 38 awards — *You're Pulling My Leg, JabberJot, Slap Wacky, Pet Detectives* and *You're Pulling My Leg Jr.* See more at MorningStarGames.com.

Great for new friends. *You're Pulling My Leg!* makes a terrific icebreaker and getting-to-know-you activity.

- Real Simple Magazine

Pet Detectives is entertaining and fun. Incorporates positive values and allows the whole family to play together.

- Stevanne Auerbach, Ph. D. "Dr. Toy"

You're Pulling My Leg Jr. teaches while challenging children to understand what makes an interesting, compelling and believable story.   *- The National Parenting Center*

Slap Wacky! is loads of fun for the whole family!   *- Parent to Parent*

ALLEN WOLF

CPSIA information can be obtained at www.ICGtesting.com
Printed in the USA
LVOW10s1507111016

508321LV00014B/1142/P